Andrew Lafleche

TRIDENT LEGION: TO CONSERVE AND PROTECT

ANDREW LAFLECHE is the award-winning poet and author of *No Diplomacy, Ride, and Spring, Summer, Winter, Fall*—among other titles. His work uses a spoken style of language to blend social criticism, philosophical reflection, explicit prose, and black comedy. Lafleche received an M.A. in Creative and Critical Writing from the University of Gloucestershire. He lives on a farmstead in the Bonnechere Valley.

www.AndrewLafleche.com

Books by

ANDREW LAFLECHE

Ashes

No Diplomacy

Shameless

A Pardonable Offence

One Hundred Little Victories

On Writing

Merica, Merica, on the Wall

After I Turn into Alcohol

Eyes Wide

Ride

Moon Poems and Other Deathless Songs

The Morning Edition

Spring, Summer, Winter, Fall

TRIDENT LEGION

To Conserve and Protect

Andrew Lafleche

Pub House Books

Montreal

Library and Archives Canada Cataloguing in Publication

Title: Trident Legion : to conserve and protect / Andrew Lafleche.
Names: Lafleche, Andrew, author.
Description: First Pub House Books edition.
Identifiers: Canadiana (print) 20220428255 | Canadiana (ebook) 20220428263 | ISBN 9781989266403
  (hardcover) | ISBN 9781989266397 (Kindle)
Subjects: LCGFT: Novels.
Classification: LCC PS8623.A3582 T75 2022 | DDC C813/.6—dc23

ISBN-13 978-1-989266-40-3

Book design by John Warden

Pub House Books
1918 Boul. Saint-Regis
Dorval, QC H9P 1H6

Printed in the United States of America

For Hudson.

Table of Contents

Chapter One: Abandon

Julian Cole woke to the dull tone of the seat belt light illuminating. It was only an hour flight from Reykjavik, but somehow he'd drifted. He looked at his friend in the seat beside him. His wavy blond hair hung neat over his shoulders as he slept peacefully against the cabin's window. In this restful state, Julian found it hard to believe he was the same Ed Barbie, twice the Trident Legion veteran, who'd deployed to the Faroe Islands and successfully intervened with the grindadrap to capture gut-wrenching video that exposed the slaughter to the world. Ed had balls.

"Sir," the stewardess said, resting her hand on Julian's arm. "It's time." She nodded at his seat belt and tilted her head toward his chair.

Julian fastened up, righted his seat, and woke his friend.

"We're about to land," Julian said.

"I couldn't sleep the entire flight from Canada to Iceland, but this short haul and I'm out cold." Ed straightened his seat and tightened his seat belt. "I hope everybody else makes it without any issues."

"We're not clear yet," Julian warned, eyebrows raised.

Ed grinned. "We'll be just fine, Jules."

And Julian believed him.

The lone airstrip, set in the farmed valley between two hills, appeared in the window. Eight isolated buildings stood in variable colours of white, red, and beige adjacent the runway. Several cars waited in the parking lot. In moments, the plane would be on the ground.

The deep northern Atlantic glittered outside the opposite windows, split only by the bright moss-green hills beneath the azure sky. Tourists murmured at the sight, unaware the beautiful ocean cove would soon be thick with blood, a brilliant red, soaking into the sand and splashing the hysterical people gathered along the shore in ritual baptismal display. Salted copper would taint each breath.

"Remember," Ed said, jarring Julian's attention from the view. "When we go through customs, make sure there are a few people between us. We can't cross over together."

"How are you even allowed back in the country? They have to know you by now."

"This will probably be the last time," Ed said. "But I'm alright with that. As soon as I get back to Canada, I've got a spot lined up on one of the ships."

"Me too," Julian said. "On the Abbey."

"No way! That's awesome. Looks like we'll be continuing the party over there."

They raised their fists and bumped them together.

"I've got another friend coming too," Ed said. "This girl, Tamara, she's insane, and apparently she's got an A.L.F. guy to join."

"A.L.F.?" Julian asked.

"Animal Liberation Front."

"Damn," Julian said, as his thoughts drifted to the allegations the Canadian Broadcasting Company had reported against the group over the years—never, not even once, had the police apprehended one of their members. Even with all the surveillance dotting New University, when the research lab was broken into, all of the mice, rats, and pigs stolen, and the entire building set ablaze. "Whoa," Julian muttered.

And Ed left it at that.

The plane touched down without incident. Some of the locals cheered as if it weren't always the case. Before the seat belt light had turned off, most of the passengers were out of their seats and pulling their luggage from the overhead bins.

"See you on the other side," Ed said, pushing past a few people and joining the shuffle off the plane.

"See you on the other side," Julian repeated, the gravity of the mission beginning to settle in his gut.

During the previous campaign, two Trident Legion volunteers were arrested and charged for interfering with the whale hunt. Intent to Obstruct Indigenous Customs was how the papers reported it. Each were given the maximum penalty of two years less a day in prison. Another volunteer was beaten unconscious by several islanders while walking home from an observation post. Of course this never earned a spot on the 6 o'clock news and is also why volunteers were never supposed to go anywhere alone. Well, except maybe to insert themselves into the country to begin with.

Julian approached the customs agent and relinquished his passport. He felt like he did the first time he had to give a speech in elementary school. His heart beat so violently Julian would swear it could be heard three custom booths over. Beads of sweat dripped down his spine beneath his shirt. He reminded himself to breathe and that most of what he was experiencing was only in his mind. He wasn't actually shaking is how his teachers would lie. Breathe.

"Welcome to the Faroe Islands," the customs agent said, returning Julian's passport.

Julian smiled. "Thank you," He said and stepped past the glass-shielded booth and uniformed official, carry-on luggage towed at his heels.

He caught up with Ed in baggage claim.

Ed laughed. "What did I tell you? That was the easy part. They look intimidating all stoic with their badge, but they're just punching the clock like everybody else." He put his arm around Julian and guided him toward the exit. "One of the crew will be outside to meet us."

The airport walls were lined with banners displaying the various must-see attractions of the Faroes: The timber-walled turf-roofed cottages of Gjogv, the glass lake over the crashing ocean, the bird cliffs and grottoes. Sunrises and sunsets casting purples over waterfalls and igniting the brilliant greens of the moss.

"They sure sell the place, don't they?" Julian asked.

"Something beautiful. Something clean. Something dramatic. Something serene," Ed said, passing beneath the plaque which arched overhead.

A shiver descended his spine. He still had nightmares of the hunt: The eruption of the villagers when a whale pod was spotted, barbaric and unmerciful. The stampede of their boots on the gravel roads as they rushed toward one of the island's seventeen designated hunting bays. The shrill revving of the small boat engines as their drivers herded the pilot whales toward the shore. The screaming of the mammals as they thrashed in the shallow waters before their spinal cords were severed by lancers, a custom-made steel spear pierced repeatedly before slitting them underneath in order to have them bleed out. How the wheelbarrows gonged hallow passing each other in haste as other locals divided the fresh meat into equal portions and slopped the carcasses into the metal bins. The frenzy contrasted by the celebration and relief of the Faroese over the success of another hunt.

Julian recited some borrowed wisdom. "All it takes for evil to prevail in the world is for good men to do nothing."

Distant, Ed asked, "Who said that?"

Julian laughed. "Someone smarter than me."

With an apathetic smile, Ed admitted, "Someone smarter than me, too."

A lanky brunette in denim overalls and a white cap-sleeved shirt paced the checkered tile floor at the bottom of the escalator. As the two guys descended closer, she beamed, winked, then curbed her smile.

"Is she one of us?" Julian asked as they stepped off.

She stuck out her hand. "I'm Lisa."

Ed slapped her hand away, hugged her close, and spun her around. Lisa squealed excitedly.

He set her down and kissed her on the cheek. "It's good to see you, Lisa."

"You guys are lucky you arrived when you did."

Ed's smile lingered. Julian shrugged. "What do you mean lucky?" he asked.

Lisa started toward the exit. "The spotters confirmed a pod of pilot whales along the coast. Our ship should be able to cut them off before the small boats get to them, but if not, we're going to need a lot of cameras rolling to capture the carnage."

Julian's face clouded with dread. "So," he started then stopped, resting his fist on his mouth.

"So, what?" Ed asked.

Before answering, Julian opened his hand and rubbed his cheek. "So, if our ship doesn't make it in time, we have to sit by and watch the slaughter? We don't do anything?"

"We get video!" Lisa snapped. She glared at him. "Is this your first campaign new guy?"

Ed raised his hand and signalled Lisa to bring it down a notch. "I get where you're coming from, man," he said. "I thought the same thing my first time out here. Obviously we want to save the whales, first priority, that's what everybody wants." He glanced at Lisa, who in turn, nodded in agreement. "It's just pretty much all of our fundraising dollars come from visuals."

"So we exploit their deaths."

"We give meaning to their deaths," Lisa corrected.

"And we're supposed to stand there with a camera and watch it all go down?" he asked, visibly perturbed.

"If you can just stand there with a camera and film without being accosted, you'll have to tell me your secret," Ed sneered jokingly.

"The Faroese smash tourist's cameras within a mile of the bay," Lisa said, mashing her fist into her hand for effect. "Not only that, if they even suspect you're with the Legion, you're in danger just being seen in public."

"Is that what happened to the guy last year?"

"Exactly," she said. "It's why we move in pairs and try only to travel to and from our positions at night."

"Julian," Ed said seriously. "You're going to learn out here that solutions are hard come by and mostly, it's just trade-offs."

Julian looked up at the sky. The sun was several hours from setting behind the western horizon. Still, clouds were advancing off the waters and a heavy fog capped the cliffs so completely their peaks appeared flat. The crisp air had the fine hair on Julian's arms standing at attention.

"Is the weather always like this?" he asked.

Lisa huffed. "Are you always this skeptical?" She looked at Ed, and in an afterthought, returned her attention to Julian. "And just so you know," she paused. "Trident Legion has been doing this a long time," her eyes narrowed. "And will be doing this long after you leave."

Julian blushed.

Ed clapped his back, and then, like a consoling teammate after a fumbled play, firmly massaged his shoulders. "Come 'on Lisa, give the guy a break. Do you remember your first deployment? I remember mine, how green I was, queasy at the position I'd found myself in. You die-hards come off a little nut-so sometimes."

Lisa cocked her hand. Ed ducked behind Julian. Everybody laughed.

"Sorry," she said. "I'm just passionate. These people and the tourists and how these whale lives are treated as sport. I get really wound up over here."

Ed straightened himself then shrugged. "I think we're all a little tense. I know none of it's personal."

"We should probably make our way," she said, and began moving again.

The three of them exited the airport. Lisa led them toward a white Ford Ranger. The truck bed was littered with scrap multi filament of green and blue and red, several five-gallon bottles of water, and a few wood-handled shovels.

Lisa took the wheel and Ed climbed into the passenger side. "You don't mind riding in the bed, do you?" he asked.

Julian scanned the items again. "Is it legal?"

The cab's window slid open with a sharp clack. Lisa shook her head at his wheedling tone. "Assume anything we do isn't legal, until we're back home."

She turned around and pounced on the gas pedal. Gravel shot from beneath the tires. Julian was tossed to the corner of the bed as the ass-end of the truck fishtailed to gain control.

The airport faded into the green grass and the buildings became dots as the team made their way to the safe-house on the outskirts of town. A not-so-secret location, but set far enough away that the natives couldn't be bothered to make the trip. Yet. Julian had the feeling if the crew success-fully intercepted the whales, the distance wouldn't stop the townspeople from coming down on them en masse. He hoped that unless there was some legitimate legal issue, their presence alone wouldn't be enough to encourage a visit from the locals. At least before they got to do something; which of course meant at least before he got to do something.

The cool fall air filled Julian's lungs. He breathed deep the fresh mountains carried by the invigorating ocean breeze. The Faroe Islands was a place still largely unmarred by the sprawl of modernity. He'd coun-ted one paved road since leaving the airport, the rest, loose gravel. There were no stoplights or billboards to impede the drive, and the houses they did pass were sparse in proximity. He thought of the fjords on the advert-isements at the airport and wondered if at some point during this cam-paign he'd be afforded the time to take in some of the attractions.

He slapped his cheek—a habit he'd started only months before and applied anytime he entertained a thought of privilege at exploiting anoth-er sentient being—he'd slap his face or punch a charlie-horse or anything that caused immediate but not excessive pain to serve as reparations for his guilty behaviour. "I love you. I'm sorry. Please forgive me. Thank you," he whispered. To no-one. To the wind. To himself. A mantra he picked up at a Tony Robins seminar he'd attended the previous year when he'd first started considering his place in the world, other species as valu-able as or even more valuable than himself. It's where he first became ve-gan and being vegan became eligible to apply to the Trident Legion. And now he was in the Faroe Islands, volunteering on a campaign that was quickly appearing to promise disaster.

Lisa pointed through the windshield. "There she is," she said, a volume just below a shout.

Julian craned his neck outside the cab and squinted against the wind.

The truck slowed. Julian focused on the hobbit home in the distance. The knoll of pine greens extended to the ocean, interrupted only by the weathered three-panel fence marking the perimeter of the property. Large boulders stood where posts could have been and were slowly being consumed by a mossy fur. The ocean swelled with caps of white and was no longer the blue seen from the sky. From here the water held a smokiness to it, livid like a weighted lead. Sea birds called in short caws before descending the cliff along the coast. The house was a pragmatic home. A stone smokestack protruded from the foot-long field grass growing on the roof. Two sky-lights fell next to the stone. The wooden eavestroughs ran into clay rain barrels below tiny windows framed in red, their shutters brown as the earth.

"It's beautiful," Julian shouted over the wind.

Lisa slapped the window in three quick claps. "They're still the enemy, remember!"

Ed winked. "Hop out and unlock the gate, will ya?"

Lisa brought the truck to a stop. Julian stumbled out of the pickup and unlatched the iron fitting. He swung the gate open. Lisa laid on the horn startling Julian, laughed, then sped down the driveway.

"She's going to be the death of me," Julian muttered, kicking at the gravel. He closed the gate, latched it shut, and walked toward the house.

He paused for a moment at the edge of the gravel and stared out to sea. The wind coming off the water brought chills. The air was rich with ocean green and brine. He inhaled deep and held his breath to invite the moist salty air to cool his core. Julian closed his eyes.

In high school, before he turned activist, his English teacher asked the class to write a paper describing their dream in life. It was a question nobody had asked him before, or since, and a question he'd completely forgotten until now. Sitting at his desk, in his grade ten homeroom English classroom, Julian closed his eyes and remembered the first time he saw that great expanse. He'd only ever visited the ocean once. It was summertime, June, in Boston. The sun burned in the blue midday sky. The water lapped lazily at his feet where he stood on the shore where the ocean met the land. Slowly, timidly perhaps, he inched forward into the chilling water. He paused for a moment when it reached his waist, but in a sudden surge of excitement he dove headlong into the swells. He remembered how the salt dried on his face while he floated on his back, his ears submerged to where the only sounds he could only hear was the heartbeat in his chest, the escaping bubbles rising to break the surface, and the fleeting garbled tones he imagined was the language of whales somewhere in the deep. Julian's dream was to one day be able to wake to the sound of the swell of the ocean: The smell of salted seaweed carried to shore by the gentle rolling waves. He would wake slowly, the translucent curtains blowing softly in the open window. He would eat fruit for breakfast and swim near the shore to invigorate his body as the headlong salt water dive had invigorate him then. After lunch, he'd siesta in the garden hammock. When he woke it was to hike, or weed, or read before dinner, forever blanketed by the starlit sky.

A stone struck Julian's calf and he flinched. He grabbed the point of impact rubbing vigorously.

"You coming inside?" Lisa called. "It's go time!"

He glared at the house, at Lisa. Ed stuck his head out the door. "The ship didn't make it to the pod before the hunters." He parried up to Lisa and hung his arm over her shoulders. He sucked his bottom lip.

Julian started toward them. He opened his mouth to reply, but Ed cut him short. "It's not an ideal way to start the campaign, but they have the whales and we need the proof." Then as an afterthought, "It will be bloody."

Julian nodded.

"You and me," he said. "We're heading up the bluff to see if we can get a perfect angle over the bay."

"I'm meeting up with the spotters," Lisa said. "We're going down on the ground to see what happens."

"How much time do we have?" He asked when he'd arrived at the steps.

"The sooner we get going the better," Lisa said. "But, I'd say, half an hour. Here," she stepped aside, "come in and grab out some gear. And get layered. It's freezing up there in the bluffs."

Ed smirked. He handed Julian a duffel bag and passed him the gear as he spoke. "Last year some of the guys got so cold," he looked at Lisa.

"Do you remember this? When Marion couldn't stop shivering so they tucked him into a nook and–"

"Blanketed him in those disgusting seabird carcasses? Yuck! I would have sooner frozen to death before I ever used those hapless birds to warm my body."

Julian was only half listening as he turned each item over in his hands before placing it in the duffel: binoculars, rope, carabiners, snap rings. A Sony camcorder.

"Sometimes you have to do what you have to do to survive," Ed said.

"Nope," she shook her head. "No way. None."

Julian looked up from the parabolic microphone he held. "Where did they get seabird carcasses? We just happen to keep those in stock?"

"No, dip," Lisa barked.

"The locals hunt the seabirds from the bluff. Big butterfly looking nets they swing over the surface of the water and snag the birds while they're diving for the fish. Once the seabirds are netted, they're swung into the rock face, knocked out, and retrieved to have their necks broken like you would a chicken."

Lisa gagged. "You're making me sick."

"It's barbaric," Ed continued. "But it's like everything out here though. They're living so far in the past they won't even entertain the idea that life could be different."

Julian's face scrunched.

Ed rubbed his eyes and massaged his temples. He took in a breath and let it go. "What I mean is, the Faroese don't consider all of these antiquated practices unnecessary in our age of enlightenment. They believe because they've always lived like this that there isn't another way, or there are no alternatives. That's why we're here. If we can just reach one Faroese native, maybe he or she can ignite the flame that will start stopping all of this killing."

Julian stuffed a blanket and two harnesses into the bag.

"Or we could just beat it into them," Lisa snarked. "Make them get with the times, expose them for the brutes they are and demand governments to force their hand."

"Yeah," Ed sighed. "Or that. It doesn't always work though."

Ed and Lisa stared at each other before mutually deciding to let their difference in opinion drop.

Julian zipped up the duffel bag. "So, they stole seabird carcasses to keep warm?"

Lisa rolled her eyes. "Jesus Julian."

The verdantly green bluffs were robed in mist. The ocean crashed against the rock in threatening overtures as the two young men struggled to locate a decent vantage point above the harbour.

"We need a nook," Ed said, eyes scanning the rock face. He pointed to a landing thirty feet below, jutting from the bluff like a conk on a tree trunk. "There."

"How are we supposed to get down there?" Julian said, more rhetorical than anything.

Ed tossed the coil of rope on the grass, knelt, and ran his hands along the surface. Julian stared but did not speak.

Ed snapped his fingers. "Knew it." He stood up and pointed at the ground. Julian shrugged. "Here," Ed said. He pulled Julian's hand down to the spot.

Julian fingered the ground apprehensively. The cold steel surprised his touch as he traced the ring overcome with moss. His apprehension was about to become fear.

"It's an anchor point," Ed explained. "Directly above the landing. I knew it was too perfect a shelf to have not been used by the locals before."

Julian tugged at the moss around the anchor and exposed the ring bolted into the rock. He shook his head and raised his brows. "It doesn't look like it's been used in years."

"It's nothing to worry about." Ed snatched the ring and gave it a firm tug. Nothing. He adjusted his fingers and yanked like it was the rip cord on a gas-operated lawnmower. "Ow!" He clenched his fist and gripped over top with his free hand. "The thing's bolted tight, Julian," he said, flexing his fingers. "We have to get down there and this is the best way. It's not anything to be worried about."

"I really don't want to do this," Julian said, shaking his head, eyes bugged.

Ed ignored him, knelt to the ring again, and pressed on the moss in either direction, fingers investigating. He stopped a foot away then tore at the greenery and exposed a second ring. "An anchor point is only as good as its second." He tugged the bolted steel with as much force as the first, winced, then set to work on the rig.

For a moment, Julian relinquished his fear and watched in admiration. Ed seemed to know a lot about, well, everything. He sighed and squatted down beside him. "What do you need me to do?" he asked.

Ed pointed to the duffel bag. "Hand me the nylon cordelette and a few carabiners."

Ed clicked two of the carabiners through the rings then knotted the ends of the nylon together to complete a circle in the rope. He twisted a fisherman's knot and set the cordelette on the ground. Two spring-loaded snaps from the carabiners signalled the line secure and the third, Ed said, meant, "Number one on rappel." He smiled. "It's easy. Besides, I'm going first. Someone has to be down there to break you if you fall."

Julian didn't even pretend to be amused, he only shook his head. "I can't do this."

"Harness up. We have to get moving."

Ed removed both safety harnesses from the duffel and handed one to Julian. With his own held out in front of him like a pair of shorts, he stepped his left foot through the left loop, then his right foot through the right and pulled the device snug around his waist. Julian found himself mirroring Ed's movements, even cinching the thigh straps, and then as if choreographed each clacked their respective belt buckles closed at the same time.

Like the veteran he was, Ed demonstrated how to thread the long rope through the anchors and the harness. He secured the rope in his right hand and tucked his fist behind his back. His left hand held loose around the guide line in front of him. He inched backward as he spoke.

"Step until there's no more ground beneath your heels, then lean."

Ed winked as he tilted over the edge and began to descend at a controlled speed. Julian peered down at him.

"And if you're feeling really adventurous," Ed hollered, "try this."

Ed crouched against the wall, knees bent, then sprung off with both feet, threw his brake hand from behind his back fully extended like a wing, and plummeted through the air above the landing. A few feet from the surface, Ed shot his hand behind his body and swung toward the rock wall, bracing his knees for impact, absorbed the shock, and pushed off gently to land upright on the shelf. It looked like he'd rappelled a hundred times before; and he probably had.

"Number one, off rappel," Ed reported, removed the rope from his harness, and flashed Julian the thumbs up.

A deep two-tone lonely cry echoed across the fogged water. The M/V Edward Abbey had arrived. The young men smiled and shifted their attention toward the sea. The fog was still too thick for a visual, but the ship had to be close to announce itself like that.

"You better get down here. Drop me the bag then thread the rope like I showed you."

Julian tied up and stepped to the edge of the bluff. Ed held the end of the rope lightly. If Julian fell, Ed would grip the rope tight, and because of the way the rope was wound through the anchor points and safety harness, Julian's swan-dive would be immediately arrested.

Even thirty feet below, the virgin rappeler's gasp could be heard as he leaned over the edge. And then it happened, the ever fatal err. Julian looked down. He released his brake hand gripping the rope securely behind his back as gravity pounced.

Julian screamed as he fell. He squeezed the line in fear. The rope snapped taut, hit him under the chin, and threw Julian flat against the wall. Ed gripped the rope with both hands and dropped to the shelf.

Julian choked, winded and panicked like a child who smacked the ground after falling from the monkey bars. The rope snapped tight from the anchors, tight across Julian's neck, tight holding his head against the rock, tight to Ed's chest who was holding fast below.

"You have to let go of the rope!" Ed yelled with an authority almost like he was prepared for this to mishap to occur.

Julian tried to speak but his lungs still didn't have air. He gagged on the palpable ocean mist.

"If you don't let go, you're going to pass out," Ed threatened, or so Julian perceived. "I have you braked from here." He motioned his head at his hands. Julian's eyes, although popped, followed Ed's direction. "I'll let you down easy. You'll float down. Scout's honour."

Julian trembled.

"Let's go Julian!"

With a final gasp, Julian closed his eyes and released his grip on the rope.

Nothing happened. It was just like Ed had promised. He hung suspended where he'd first collided with the rock face. Then slowly, very slowly, Ed let out centimetre after centimetre of rope, lowering Julian gently toward the landing. When finally safe on the shelf, he laid on his back and rubbed his neck.

"I told you I didn't want to do that," he whined.

Ed pointed at the lump of young man on the ground. "You didn't follow my instructions," he said and shook his head. "This one's on you."

Julian removed his hand from his neck. Splotches of red dotted his palm. He showed it to his friend.

Ed nodded. "It's going to hurt for a while, right over the collar line and all. But," he paused, a big grin appearing on his face. "Look at it this way: You just earned your first battle scar. Chicks dig dudes with scars. They're like magnets." Still smiling, he rolled up his sleeve to expose two star-shaped explosions scarred on his bicep. Julian winced.

"Yeah," he started. "From when we were pulling up an abandoned long line in Panama. It was coming in easy enough when the bosun spotted a black spot rising in the water. You have to be careful with these lines because there are six-inch hooks every five feet." He stood knees bent, hands clenched and outstretched. "So, I'm holding the line, wearing my gloves to avoid getting sliced, and the shadow we thought was a dead animal, lurched, then breached the surface like an angry pike, only it was the ocean so a reef shark, dove back under and yanked the line from our grip. I was lucky we had it on the windlass or the jerk would have took my whole arm off with him."

"Jesus," Julian sighed, rubbing his own bicep, momentarily forgetting the burn on his neck.

"Yours will heal, just like mine did, everything does in time. Don't worry. Besides, climbing up is a lot easier than rappelling down."

"There has to be a better way."

Ed shook his head. "Pass me the binos."

"What?"

"The binoculars," Ed said, almost sounding annoyed. "The Abbey is close and we need eyes on."

Julian propped himself on his elbows, turned his head in either direc-tion and slowly pushed himself to standing. He moseyed through the duffel and produced a pair of Bushnell binoculars.

Ed sat, dangling his feet over the edge of the landing, and scanned the harbour's entrance. He traversed his arcs, left and right, left and…"Grab a seat boy," he said, patting the rock floor beside him. "Help is on the way."

He passed the binoculars and pointed in the direction of the incoming ship.

"It's here!" Julian cried. "The Abbey is really here." Then as an after-thought he admitted, "I've only ever seen it in pictures."

The 110-foot Coast Guard Cutter, refurbished and named the Edward Abbey, motored into view. The unmistakable twelve-foot skull and cross-bones painted black below the bridge, stole through the fog. A pirate ship of Robin Hood persuasion.

"It's beautiful," he whispered.

Ed snatched the binoculars back. He panned the deck looking for old friends. The weathered grip-tape surface bubbled from years of neglect by untrained volunteer crew. Rust streaked the white hull. The life rings hung in place along the bulkheads, but their lines were tangled and the ones which still had glow lights attached, their bulbs were shattered or missing. Hatches were propped open; doors the same. Two quick swells and there would be enough water taken on board to sink the ship and all its crew. A straight plunge direct to Davy Jones' locker with nothing any-body could do to stop it. Ed smiled. As haphazard as the entire operation was, somehow, they always managed to survive. Everything was exactly how he remembered it.

The crane flaked lurid iron russet and its cable was frayed from being kept exposed to the corrosive conditions of the sea. Its cover was tucked behind the exhaust, disintegrating from the heat of the engines. Drills and disc-grinders and various screwdrivers and hoses were scattered across the deck where presumably someone had been working but had now abandoned their task. The life rafts sat neglected, faded and hidden under mountains of netting making them impossible to reach in case of emer-gency. The latches securing the rafts to the launch were seized with rust. A derelict jet-ski commanded most of the square-footage of the aft-deck.

"Do you see that jet-ski?"

Julian nodded.

"We used to use it to transport crew from shore to sea and back, but this Mexican, Rodriguez, didn't know what he was doing and overloaded the thing with three people and a set of luggage. Halfway to shore he tipped it into the drink." Ed laughed recollecting the circus. "Rody didn't even know how to swim, splashing about, hooting and screaming and hollering in Spanish. Buddy with him nearly had to punch him in the face and knock him out just to get him calmed down enough to pull him back on the machine. You can bet the captain put an end to that real quick. They probably haven't even used it since." Ed passed the binos to Julian and stood up. "Well," he said. "We better get the camera ready."

They huddled over the duffel. Ed pieced the video camera and para-bolic mic together. "Footage is one thing," he said as he worked. "But like Lisa pointed out, if you can get the screams of the mammals as they're being bludgeoned to death, the calves desperate cries for their dead famil-ies as they swim for hours in the bloodied waters, well, that's pay dirt."

Julian didn't know whether to chuckle or puke. He shook the image off and raised his hands. "What do I do?"

"Just keep the mic pointed on the action."

An iron bleat and two bursts of an air raid siren lurched from sea. Both young men jumped and smarted their attention. They peered through the fog. And then they saw it. Masked near perfect with the gloomy day and swelling waters, the matte death grey of the Royal Danish Navy Iver frigate stood stoic in the harbour's entrance. The bridge of a dozen frozen black windows glared piercingly, adorned with floodlights, a radar, and a mast toting 50mm cannons trained directly on the Edward Abbey. They gasped in unison.

"This can't be good," Julian said. Ed only stared.

It's illegal to interfere with the hunt, the grindadrap. With the Trident Legion having campaigned in the Islands for several years now, it was only a matter of time before the community decided to hand the fight over to the big guns. Literally.

The Abbey slowed to a drift. The frigate opened its starboard bay door and revealed two Riverine Command Boats, black and mean as an alley after midnight. A crane lowered the vessels into the sea. Their engines roared like squealing chainsaws about to slay a hundred-year-old oak tree. The RCB's opened their throttles and exploded in tandem toward the Edward Abbey.

"Are you recording?" Julian asked.

"Just keep aiming the mic," Ed said, eyes trained on the viewfinder as he manipulated the zoom for a clearer shot.

The Abbey's captain exited the bridge and stood above the deck's main ladder. She held her hands firm to her hips, elbows akimbo. Jessie Treeville, the legendary six-foot-four Trident Legion superstar. The same Jessie who only two years prior was arrested and deported from Japan for commandeering a rigid-hull inflatable, pursued a fleet of whaling ships, while hurling thick eight-inch braided ropes twelve-feet in length at the ships' propellers to earn three different prop fouls, jamming the whaling fleet's propellers and forcing them off the chase in order to tend the damage.

Ed smiled. "She's not going to go down without a fight."

The RCB's tied up on either side of the ship, secured their own ladders to the stanchions, and ran the steps with military precision, their matte black carbines gripped tight in one hand, their free hands pointed in the direction they were travelling. The boarding team dispersed along the port and starboard fore and aft-decks, clearing each square-foot of free space. They kept their guns trained on each companionway and open hatches.

None of the Abbey's crew emerged.

"What's happening?" Julian asked.

Ed raised his finger to his lips.

The static of intercom reverberated above the water. The mother ship, the Iver frigate, cleared its throat.

One of the soldiers in the boarding crew barked a command at the Abbey's captain. Jessie slowly dropped to her knees and placed her hands on her head. Ed shook his own in disbelief.

"This is Admiral Michiel Adriaenszoon de Ruyter of the Royal Danish Navy, you are illegally operating in Faroese territorial waters." A squelch crackled with his pause. "We are forced to take control of your vessel and escort your crew to shore where they will be arrested and taken into custody."

Ed shrank to his knees and murmured, "No, no, no, no, no."

The Admiral continued. "Jessie Treeville," he said sternly.

If Jessie was surprised at being singled out, her face did not quiver. Even on her knees, fingers interlaced behind her head, Jessie remained stone. She lived for action.

"You are being relieved of your command. The Lieutenant will now place you under arrest in violation of maritime law. You will be handcuffed and escorted from the Edward Abbey, immediately."

Two soldiers ran the ladder. The balaclava wearing bosun pushed Jessie face down then the Lieutenant handcuffed her. The two men hoisted her to her feet and shuffled her down the stairs. They seated her in the starboard RCB, which detached from the ship and accelerated toward the frigate. The remaining navy team sealed the companionways and hatches. Several of them stayed on deck, carbines relaxed, while the others secured the bridge—and presumably the rest of the Legion crew below—in preparation to bring the ship to shore.

Two short pulls of the frigate's air horn and the M/V Edward Abbey began a slow exit from the harbour. When it cleared the entrance and disappeared behind the rocks, an eerie silence descended on the bay. It was as if the waves had stopped crashing on the bluff. The wind had tapered into a gentle breeze. Only the reflexive fog remained unchanged.

Ed and Julian sat in disbelief.

"What do we do now?" Julian asked.

"We climb."

Julian's face sheeted white. His hands shook a little.

"The R.O.E.'s say we go back to the house."

"R.O.E.'s?"

"Rules of…" Ed paused. "I don't know. Get up. You're going first in case of last time."

Julian thread the lead line through his belt. He pressed one foot against the bluff and stopped.

"Just walk," Ed said, this time certainly annoyed. "Don't let go and don't stop until you reach the top."

His trembled as he leaned back and stepped his other foot. One at a time he started to walk. Ed gripped the rope in anticipation of a fall, but a fall never happened. Once Julian had cleared the ridge, Ed picked up the slack and stepped confidently into position.

"We're screwed," Julian said.

Ed quick marched up the wall. "Take the harness off and be prepared to go home," he said climbing over the ledge.

"We're not leaving already."

"They commandeered our ship." Ed scowled. "What are we supposed to do?"

The two removed their safety harnesses and returned them to the bag. Ed strapped the duffel to his back and walked toward the hobbit cabin they'd only just arrived from.

Julian puffed up his bottom lip and shook his head. "I'm not going back to Canada—we can't quit."

"So stay here by yourself." Ed didn't look back. "We can't afford to lose everybody over a single ship. We have at least a dozen people here."

Julian started after Ed. "And we're running away."

"Just fly, Julian, you're already guaranteed a spot in Mexico when you get back." He snarled over his shoulder. "This mission is over."

Julian couldn't believe his ears. He thought about the Trident Legion he'd seen on TV, how they always fought fire with some of their own, throwing acid, scuttling boats, preparing to ram! They wouldn't quit over a minor setback. Fast and cheeky he quipped, "Maybe we should wait for your girlfriend before we chicken out." He didn't get a response so he tried again. "She probably knows more being here before you and all." Nothing. Julian picked up a stone, round and smooth, and threw it at Ed. It bounced off his jacket. If Ed felt it, he didn't let on.

Chapter Two: Collapse

The hobbit home appeared over the knoll. Lisa's 4x4 was parked beside two other Ford Rangers, each of them white. Warm exhaust rose from the mufflers as each vehicle idled. People shuffled to and from the house carrying various sized duffels and hard-shelled Pelican cases. Ed hastened into a light jog. He looked over his shoulder, nodded his head as if to say, "Come 'on now."

Julian rolled his eyes. "They can't be serious," he muttered. Julian sighed then began jogging to keep up with his partner. His quitter partner. A whole organization of quitters as far as Julian was concerned.

They arrived at the house together. The scene had Julian believe maybe Ed wasn't being a coward after all, that there might actually be a real threat. Crew members bumped into each other as they scrambled back and forth to collect the most important gear. Hard cases were dropped, "Those drones cost thirty-grand!" Flash drives and memory cards bounced out of bins, "Crap-crap-crap-crap-cra-cra-crap," while other crew fell to their knees to scour the grass ensuring none of the tiny plastic sticks were left behind. Several volunteers were glared at, "Six months of footage they're just tossing around haphazardly." Someone cursed, "I can't wait to get away from these land crew. They're useless." Others narrowed their eyes and mumbled under their breath. Lisa dashed through the hive of people. She skirted the crew combing the grass, and aimed herself directly at Ed.

"You don't answer your radio?" she screamed in her advance.

Ed stopped, raised his hands slightly, and cocked his head. He stood perfectly still. His focused demeanour forced Julian to wonder if the situation was something to be worried about.

Lisa fumed, face red, heavy breath, laser stare. "I've been calling you for hours! I was sure they got to you." Tears welled in her eyes. "You're such an arse." She pounded his chest.

He wrapped his arms around her. "I'm okay," Ed whispered. He rubbed her back gently. "Everything's okay."

Julian blushed and rolled his eyes. "Gross," he whined.

Lisa ripped herself from Ed, raised her fist above her head, and screamed a warrior scream so loud Julian jumped back unsure whether he should be fearing for his life. Ed caught her by the elbow.

"Enough Julian." Ed glared at him. Thirty seconds passed before he spoke again, this time to Lisa. "He doesn't take anything serious."

That stung, but he didn't engage. His pouty tantrum quickly evaporated, and in his new seriousness he asked, "What do you need me to do?"

Lisa turned back to the house, but not before berating him. "Stay out of the way," she barked, not looking back.

Ed took a deep breath, relaxed his posture, faced Julian, and rested both hands on his shoulders.

"It's not like that," he started. "Just most of the crew have done this before." The flow of traffic to and from the house had tapered off and people were now loading into the vehicles. "They look done. Why don't you bring our bag to the truck, I'll check inside, we should be about ready to go."

Julian nodded. He picked up the duffel and sulked his way to the truck.

"Hey," Ed hollered. Julian looked back. "I'm sorry for getting onto you. This isn't how I pictured the campaign to go, and, I let my emotions get in the way for a minute." He sighed. "You're a good kid. It would have been fun to get it on over here; but there's always Mexico, right? I'm looking forward to having you on the ship with us. I think we'll do some good down there." Ed tucked his lips to offer a sincere smile. Then he shook his head and grinned huge. "Just stop messing with Lisa." He laughed. "She's wound up enough."

Julian smirked. "Alright, alright." He resumed his walk. "Not even once a day?" he joked.

Ed waved him away, shaking his head. He mumbled something that sounded like, "Just once a day," but Julian couldn't be sure.

The two other trucks pulled out and sped off down the gravel road which he, Ed, and Lisa had travelled earlier in the day. The trucks were consumed in a cloud of dust before they broke the crest and descended the hill.

Julian tossed the duffel into the bed of the Ford and climbed in after it. He sat against the back of the cab and picked at the multi filament netting which littered the floor. His thoughts drifted out to sea and settled on the shadowed pod of pilot whales approaching certain death. Julian thought about the fuel the Abbey burned on the voyage over and cringed. He looked to the hill the trucks had disappeared behind, their exhausted dust clouds settling like a weighted fog. He loathed the ten-hour return flight, the ten-hour flight he'd only just arrived on, all the fuel that airplanes burn. For a conservation outfit, they sure do their part in keeping the oil industry afloat.

"What a waste," he said out to nobody. He rolled the multi filament he was fingering into a tight little ball and flicked it over the side of the cab.

"Are you still whining back there?" Julian jumped at the voice come from nowhere suddenly beside him. Lisa rolled her eyes. "You're going to have a stroke if you keep that up."

Julian straightened himself. He didn't want to react this time. Disappointed as he was, he didn't have it in him. All he wanted to do now was go home. "Do you think they'll let us leave?" Julian asked.

"We came in legally; we're leaving without having done anything."

The way she lingered on anything, Julian thought it almost sounded like she was trying to empathize with how he was feeling. Almost.

She shrugged. "They'll be happy to see us go."

Ed approached. "Same as when we got here, buddy. We'll go through customs one at a time and meet on the other side." He thumbed a tooth for a moment, spit something, then continued, "This isn't a failure, Julian. A disappointment for sure, but it's about longevity. Knowing when to push and knowing when to pull back—we don't have to win every campaign to take the set, you know?"

Lisa hummed along. "We've been here years now, hunt after hunt, the world knows. You were here—"

"But I didn't do anything," Julian whined.

"You showed up. You responded to the call. That's more than most people are willing to do. Everybody has their excuse not to, that's for sure. You'll get yours." She grinned, cheeks raised, corners of mouth stretched devilishly to each ear. "I promise you that."

They took their seats in the truck and Lisa punched it into reverse. Julian flattened against the cab and sighed. "I hope so," he said and watched as the sea disappeared into their own cloud of dust and exhaust.

Chapter Three: Liberation

Tawd Rawlings crouched behind the Zoological Society sign, outside of the San Diego Zoo, concealed by manicured palms and cycads. Two life-size topiary elephants, complete with artificial tusks, towered behind him. The last of the sun-baked tourists limped by with their gift shop bags stuffed with plush tigers and rainbow t-shirts manufactured in Malaysia and shipped to gift shops around the world for impulse purchases and quick disposal.

Tawd bit his lip then hung his head. He glanced at his watch. Twenty minutes until closing. The workers would filter out ten minutes later and the sun would set shortly thereafter. Tawd placed the small roll of carpet he'd brought with on the ground and took a seat. He rubbed his face. She should have been here by now.

A shrill, prepubescent voice distracted his thought.

"Daddy," the boy said. "Did you see me making faces at the gorilla, how he beat his chest at me?"

The father grinned, clapped a hand to the boy's back, and tipped his head. "He looked mad."

"We should come back and see if we can get the crocodiles to snap at us!"

"Maybe next weekend," the father said as they continued out of earshot.

Tawd hated the thought but had convinced himself it was true: Zoos are animal prisons peddled as a pleasure to be enjoyed by the public.

The grass rustled, but before he could react, a Kentia Palm slapped him across the cheek, sudden and stinging as a backhand.

Tamara dropped to her bare knees next to him and placed her hands on his reddened face. "Sorry. I didn't think you were back here yet."

Tawd pushed her hands away and scrubbed his face himself. "That hurt."

Tamara shrugged like 'what's done is done,' and shuffled onto the carpet beside him. "Shove a bum, chum."

He let out a deep sigh. "You were supposed to be here twenty minutes ago."

She snapped her head around and narrowed her eyes. "Is this really how you want to start the night?" Tamara adjusted herself on the roll. "I said I was sorry." She took a can of red spray paint from her knapsack and shook it a couple times. The little weighted ball clattered against its aluminum walls.

Tawd snatched it from her. "You're going to give away our hiding spot."

"Relax, man. I thought you'd be excited. We're finally doing something people will have to notice."

He set the spray paint beside his roll. "Maybe you're right," he said. "I'm sorry. For real. I don't know what's going on with me. Just before you got here, I overheard this kid bragging to his dad about harassing the gorillas and wanting to come back to do the same to the crocodiles. And the dad was encouraging it. As if all the animals inside these cages aren't sentient but simply mere attractions. As if none of their lives matter."

Tamara stared blankly at Tawd.

"These things really piss me off!" Tawd punched the ground. "Who are we to say our lives are more important than animal lives? That's speciesism. You don't see zebras building skyscrapers or chimpanzees raping the oceans. That's us. People ruin everything. They're disgusting and they're becoming more ignorant by the hour. So bad I can't even walk down the street without turning Hulk and having to force Kundalini breathing so I don't rage out."

"It's aquariums that trigger me," Tamara said in earnest. "I can't even count the number of restaurants I've been thrown out of for losing it on the server when I realized there were actual fish tanks in the building."

"I need to get out of the city," he said. "But it's not like I can just take off. Besides you there isn't anybody around here doing anything to make a difference."

The zoo's main lights clicked off. Tawd and Tamara flinched. Little smiles stole the corners of each of their mouths.

"Showtime," Tamara said.

"Just about," Tawd replied. Keeping in the foliage, Tawd peered out toward the front gate. Several employees stood huddled near the ticket window. "Soon as the last worker leaves, we're good."

"We should have brought some rope and tied them up."

"Yeah, because if they ever did a line-up, they'd never pick a tatted six-foot white male with dreads hung to his crack and a five-foot nothing white female with pink streaks in her hair."

"White. White. White. It's 2015, man," Tamara said. "You have to drop that race business."

"Are you kidding me? The white patriarchy is exactly what we need to be exposing."

"Uh-huh. How do you justify your dreads? I mean that's appropriation, isn't it?"

"I never should have invited you."

As the last of the employees drove away, Tamara noticed a single car in the parking lot. "Night security?"

"Yeah, just the one guy. But he patrols the same way each night, and the lemur cage is either at the start of his route, or the end, so once we're over the wall we'll just make sure he's passed by or moving in the other direction."

"And we'll have about an hour?"

"Yeah, but we won't need it."

They shuffled under the plants, out of the foliage, and looked both ways along the path between the zoo and the car park. With all clear they darted to the section of wall adjacent the ticket booth.

"I'm going to lift you," Tawd said. "Then you lay the carpet over the barbed wire."

"Wuss."

"Do it without the rug then."

"You still won't light up, will you?" Tamara lifted her foot to step into Tawd's clasped hands. "If you have a heart attack on the other side of this wall, there's no way I'll be able to lift you back over."

Tawd smiled. "Alright," he said. "Up you go."

Tawd lifted her into the air. Tamara laid the rug on the ledge and climbed over. Then Tawd stepped back a few feet and with a running start, kicked off the wall and pulled himself up. "Heart attack my arse," he mumbled in between catching his breath." He straddled the wall then lowered himself to the other side.

"Where are the wire cutters?" Tamara asked.

Tawd lifted his shirt above his waist. Two handles jutted from his pant line.

"And my spray paint?"

"I left it in the bushes."

"Tawd!"

"You're not writing some liberation message. We're not supposed to exist, remember?"

"You're such a jerk."

Tawd crept to the main walkway and looked toward the giraffe house. Nothing. He looked the other way toward the lemurs. "I don't see the se-curity guard anywhere," he whispered.

Tamara edged toward him and squinted in both directions. "There," she said, pointing down the path. "You can see his flashlight bouncing off the shrubs."

"Perfect. The lemurs are the other way."

Tamara followed Tawd along the edge of the path. She looked over her shoulder every three steps to make sure the security guard hadn't turned around. When she bumped into Tawd, not realizing he'd stopped at the exhibit, she gasped. "Sorry," she murmured.

"All good. You're up anyways."

Tamara removed a thin felt pouch from her pocket, pulled back the loose fitted flap, and shook out two thin strips of metal; one bent in the shape of an L, the other straight and plain except for the jagged teeth ground into one end. She knelt at the entrance to the trainer building.

"They really taught you this in circus school?"

"You wouldn't believe the stuff they taught us. I can deep-throat a beer can."

"I can't believe there's such thing as circus school."

She picked at the lock with her tools. The clicking pins and pressured springs seemed to echo through the zoo. She sucked on her lip as she worked.

"I thought you knew what you were doing," Tawd scoffed. He shuffled his feet. "Let's go let's go let's go."

"Chill, dude. It's not like in the movies. I'll get it in a sec." She shifted to her other knee and continued to work.

Tawd scanned the path. He couldn't see the security guard's bouncing flashlight beam and assumed he was on the return route. "Maybe there's another door."

Tamara smirked then clicked the lock over. "Got it." She pushed the door open and stepped into the unlit room. The pungent air was heavy and hinted of damp fur not quite eradicated by the sterile bitterness of medical cleaning supplies.

"I'll find a crate and you start with the exhibit, yeah?" she said.

Tawd nodded. He closed the door behind them, then followed the wall to the back of the room where the exhibit entrance was located. Tamara flicked on her flashlight. She ran her hand along the steel counter as she scanned the shelves for a transport crate.

"Poor things," she whispered to herself, thinking of all the animals that had been treated in cold, stale rooms like this one. Born in captivity, never knowing, never experiencing what it was like to live free, to be free, to be wild.

She wanted to spray the walls in capital letters: M-U-R-D-E-R-E-R-S. She felt her pockets for lipstick but didn't feel anything. At the far end of the counter, on the wall, hung a white, rectangular cabinet. A key jutted from the lock and the way its round edges revealed the brass beneath the nickle plating suggested that after it first entered the slot, the key had never been removed. A smile crept over her face. She opened the cabinet and stood stunned at the sight.

Prozac. Valium. Haldol. An entire catalogue of psychotropic pharmaceuticals which people used to sedate themselves, and here they were, stock and ready management tools for the staff to sedate their prisoners. She shoved as many of the bottles as she could into her pockets. When she found the transport crate she joined Tawd in the exhibit.

The path's streetlamps cast shadows over the arranged branches and polished boulders, settling in an eerie twist of graveyard impersonation. The usually emerald moat swelled cauldron black. The hickory wigwam set atop the hill in the centre of the enclosure, home to the two lemurs, looked like a WWII machine gun nest. Grated steel fencing guarded the enclosure.

Tamara shivered and focused her attention on Tawd. "You'll never believe what I found inside." She took a bottle from her pocket and tossed it at him.

He caught it with surprising agility. "Oh yeah," he said. "They've been using all types of drugs to keep the animals lethargic: antidepressants, tranquilizers, anti-psychotics. It's unreal. Valium for the gorillas, Haldol for the zebras." Tawd spit on the ground. "Someone needs to burn this place down."

Tamara nodded, took the bottle back, and handed Tawd the crate.

"I'll open the fence and guide the lemurs over," Tawd said. "As soon as they're both in the crate, just slide the panel down until it clicks. They shouldn't freak out. It's the same way they're brought in for treatments and whatever so–"

A door slammed. Tawd and Tamara froze.

Tamara mouthed her words but did not speak. "What was that?"

In ultra slow motion they crouched and crept along the shrubbery until they were leaning against the wall of the trainer building. Tawd slid his hand across his throat. "Maybe we should abort this."

"No way," Tamara said harshly. "I need this."

They settled onto the ground and waited.

Lights flooded the exhibit. The green water in the moat rippled gently. A pair of blinking orange eyes peaked out of the wigwam. A second pair appeared beside the first. Tamara and Tawd held their collective breath.

A dull creak slipped from inside the building.

They listened harder, mouths ajar, ears cocked toward the door.

Tiny clinks of pills being poured on the metal counter echoed inside the walls. The echo was replaced by a staccato drumming recognizable by anyone who has ever chopped pills before. Tamara chuckled.

"It's that security guard," she whispered. "He's raiding the drug cabinet."

Tawd held a finger to his lips.

She rolled her eyes.

The drumming stopped. Both of them waited for the inevitable rough and forceful nostrilling sniff. And it sounded right on cue. The lights extinguished. The door opened and slammed again. The lock turned over and the flashlight beam resumed its bounce along the path toward the giraffes, a quiet but joyful whistle bobbing along with it.

Tawd and Tamara slumped against the wall. When they couldn't see the light any longer, Tamara spoke. "What are the chances, right?"

"That could have been very, very bad." He wagged his head.

"It's almost like the clock is reset though. He's going to walk all the way around before getting back."

"I want to know how he got here so quick when the last time we saw him he was walking the other direction."

Tamara shrugged. "Let's just grab these guys and get lost."

Tawd opened the gate and stepped inside the lemur enclosure. He removed the long pole from its place on the fence. A loop of cord hung from one end, the kind of loop that tightens when pulled to cinch around the neck of the animal. He didn't like the idea of it, but also knew it was the only way to set the captives free. Temporary measures.

"I'll be gentle," he said in the direction of the staring eyes.

Tamara shone her flashlight and the little orange dots squeezed shut. Tawd held the pole and slipped the rope around the neck of one of the lemurs. He pulled lightly. The lemur didn't resist. Instead, the furry creature trotted along as it was led toward the exit. They locked him in the transport crate and Tawd returned for the second. Clockwork. Easy as the first. One cage to the other. He set the pole onto its hooks and used his sleeve to wipe it clean. Tamara was already inside the building, holding the door for Tawd.

"That was easy," she said.

Tawd winked. With their newly acquired lemurs she started toward the wall they'd first climbed over with the rug. Tawd caught her by the arm and pulled her back.

"No chance we'll get over the wall with these guys," he said, holding up the crate.

"So, what? We just go out the front gate?"

"Exactly."

"Won't that set off an alarm?"

"You're not the only one with tricks up your sleeve," Tawd said. "I'll handle the alarm."

They shuffled along the wall keeping an eye out for the night watchman. The lemurs stirred, shifting their weight side-to-side making it difficult to keep the crate balanced. They'd squeal soon enough. Tamara stopped at the front gate and leaned against the tall iron bars. She felt a bulge in her pocket and remembered the pills.

"Do you want a Valium?" she asked, pulling the bottle from her pocket.

"No!" He stared at her, mouth ajar and shook his head. "I don't want a Valium."

"It's not Ambien, dude," she said. "If I was your doctor, you'd have been on Valium years ago."

"Keep watch, will ya?" Tawd said. "That guard could be back any second."

Tawd set the crate on the ground and climbed onto the handrail, balancing himself on the iron bars. He pulled something from his pocket and slid it between the two white rectangles above.

"All there is to it," he said. "Twenty-five cent fridge magnet and you can get past any alarm system."

"You're joking."

"Serious as a heart attack," he said. "Here." Tawd waved at Tamara. "I'll even let you open the gate."

"So if the alarm goes off you can blame me?"

"So you'll know why I'm so confident."

"Why do guys do that?" she said.

"Do what?"

"Brag about your smarts as if you're all a bunch of little Einsteins?"

"Just open it."

Tamara pushed the crash bar on the gate and slowly stepped through the entrance. Tawd followed with their newly liberated lemurs.

"Now what?" Tamara asked.

"Close the gate. Home free."

But before Tamara closed the gate fully, the magnet slipped. She watched time stop. They snapped eyes at each other, mouths gaped, and dashed toward the parking lot.

The alarm blared, sharp as a schoolyard fire bell.

The lemurs screamed in their crate. Tawd sprinted toward the far corner of the fencing. Tamara held her pockets as she ran, pill bottles shaking like maracas. They reached the shadowed corner and fell against the fence. The lemurs shook in shock, screams arrested to a droning whine.

"Not good," Tawd uttered, hunched over holding his knees.

Out of breath, Tamara rested her hands on her head. "Where did you park?"

"You mean my hot dog cart?"

"What?" Tamara snapped. "No! Why would I care where you parked your hot dog cart? Your car. You know, the getaway vehicle!"

"Getaway vehicle? You know I don't drive. I just have the pedal bike on my cart. My carbon footprint is virtually zero."

"Seriously?" Tamara yanked her hair. "We need to get out of here, like, now."

She began climbing the fence. Tawd grabbed the back of her jacket and tugged her down. Before she could cuss him, Tawd lifted the edge of the chain-link closest the steel pole. It rolled open.

Tamara slipped through and Tawd followed.

"We'll cross over into the golf course and disappear there," Tawd said. "Don't stop running until we break the tree line. You ready?"

Tamara inhaled deeply. Her face was no longer lighthearted and jovial as it had been the entire operation. She was pale, eyes bugged, lips tight.

"I can't go to jail, Tawd."

He looked her in the eyes and placed his hands on her shoulders. "Nobody's going to jail, Tamara. Trust me." He nodded his head and waited for her to return the gesture. "Are you ready? I need you to run with me."

He crept up to the road and waited for the lone car driving the main drag to pass through the intersection. "Now," he whispered sharply.

He ran into the street, lemurs screaming in terror, Tamara immediately to his rear. Tawd's hair leapt with each stride. Tamara rattled a fierce rainstorm of pills in her pockets.

Across the street, they dashed into the ditch, over the sidewalk, and behind the tree line. They'd made it.

The lemurs calmed as Tawd and Tamara walked the golf course trails.

"So, what are you going to do with these guys?" Tamara asked.

"I have a cousin who said he could get them into a conservation area."

"Here in the States?"

"Yeah," Tawd said. "It's not ideal. I'd want them returned to the wild, but they're tame now. Even in conservation space there's a chance they might not survive."

"At least they'll experience being free."

"Maybe. The zoo is just going to buy more lemurs, though."

"We do our best and forget the rest," Tamara said.

"There's just so much to do and nobody's doing anything. Not Greenpeace, not the Animal Liberation Front, nobody."

"What about the Trident Legion?"

"What about them?"

"You've seen the show. Whale Wars. How they mess with the Japan-ese and poachers and are actually still doing stuff. If you're serious, I can get you an interview with their recruiter. I'm leaving for a campaign in a couple of weeks."

Tawd mulled the offer in his head.

"You'd just have to give up your little hot dog stand," she teased.

"Vegan hot dog stand," Tawd corrected.

Chapter Four: Introduction

Three months had passed since the Trident Legion retreated from the Faroe Islands. Julian's bruised pride had had time to heal where now he was itching to get back on campaign. Restless. The call finally came and with his bags already packed he boarded another flight, this time to Mexicali, the capital city of Baja California, Mexico. On arrival he bought a seat on a bus crammed with local nationals and travelled three hours through the mountainous desert terrain to arrive in San Felipe. Unable to speak Mexico's native language, Julian hoped that some of the crew would be waiting at the bus depot for him when the bus pulled up.

The air stood in layers atop dusted gravel in the depot parking lot. Julian squinted at the sun as he stepped from the bus. Compared to the crisp cool air of the Faroes, Mexico may as well have been the Sahara Desert. Beads of sweat formed on his forehead, which he quickly wiped away with his forearm. It's important to deny the heat in an attempt to trick the mind into believing that the heat isn't unbearable and pretend the sun isn't a complete jerk along the more regrettable latitudes. With a heavy breath Julian scanned the crowd of reunited travellers for anyone who might be Trident Legion. When the last of the passengers retrieved their luggage, the driver closed the door, locked it, and disappeared inside the nondescript, vacant-looking the building. Julian set his backpack on the curb and sat on it. The bus's air brake hissed. A smell of smouldering garbage, melting plastics, and burnt papers wafted by. He cringed.

Julian ground his foot in the mustard-brown dirt and watched the plume of dust rise and fall. He sighed. Nobody. No cellphone. No idea where he was. No Spanish to support him. All he could do was wait. Someone would come for him. They said that they would. They had to.

"Las Claritas," he read the sign mounted below a boarded-up vendor booth. "Las Claritas," he said again. The tin roof was streaked in rust, uneven and twisted with age. The fence that surrounded the booth, its paint a faded sky blue, weaved together like a warped lattice arbour. It was a miracle it stood erect at all. Both adjoining buildings had bars mounted over their windows and heavy gatehouse style steel doors securing their entrances. Palms grew along the road. Their lower branches were brown and drooping. The highest limbs were green and skyward. None of them had any coconuts.

Julian didn't notice the Ford pickup approach and park beside the bus. He jumped when a familiar voice called his name.

Ed laughed from the passenger seat. "Still on edge as ever."

Julian simpered. He hadn't heard from Ed since the early departure from the GrindStop campaign, and he was sure hoping Ed would be here when he arrived for the start of Milagro. Even if Ed did find pleasure in riling him up.

"Are you just going to sit there grinning like an idiot, or you going to mount up?" Ed teased. "We have work to do."

Julian tossed his backpack into the truck bed and crawled over the side. It instantly felt a whole lot like the Faroes except this time it wasn't a lanky brunette behind the steering wheel. This driver filled the seat, dreads swaying to his knees, tattoos covering everything except his cheeks and ears which seemed to be reserved for enough piercings to set off the scanner at airport security ten departures back.

The man reached his paw through the sliding window. "I'm Tawd," he said, voice more youthful than his appearance. "Just like it sounds, T-A-W-D." He paused, as if he'd done this before and enjoyed the confused reaction that scrunched the brow of whoever happened to be on the re-ceiving end of this rehearsed speech, a pause which demanded, 'What? You've never heard Tawd spelled that way before?'

Julian shook his outstretched hand, unsure how to respond.

"You better hold on back there," Tawd laughed. "These roads are bumpy as all hell."

Ed smirked. "And Tawd drives like a maniac."

"Only because I haven't driven in years."

Julian barely gripped the bedside panels when Tawd squealed the rear-wheel-drive into reverse, tapped the brakes, then dropped the beat-up pickup truck into gear, racing out of the parking lot and jumped onto the weathered desert road.

Even at speed, the coastal Baja air maintained its oppressiveness. Julian covered his face with his hands, mouth and nose mostly, as dust flooded the bed like a tsunami before crashing into the windscreens of the other vehicles behind. Drivers honked their horns. Brake lights flashed. Tawd raced along.

Julian slipped his shirt off and tied it around his face. His hands weren't doing anything to keep the dust from clamming up his breathing holes.

Ed popped his head through the glass and laughed.

"You sure like pairing up with cowboys," Julian hollered over the sound of the wind and ricocheting stones.

"How have you been?" Ed said.

"Just waiting, man," Julian said. "When did you get here?"

"They flew me down a few weeks after we left the island."

Julian flinched. Ed had already been here two months and he had only just gotten the call now?

Ed chuckled. "Lisa's going to be thrilled to see that you're still super easy to get wound up."

"I just can't believe you've been here that long and I'm just getting here now."

"Nine weeks, actually."

Julian disapproved, but, at least he was back in the action.

"You said we have work to do," Julian said. "What's up?"

Tawd spun the wheel to the left and fishtailed down a paved side street. "Almost missed that one!" he yelled, not taking his eyes off the road. "Hold on!"

He tapped the brakes a few times and spun the steering wheel in the other direction. The tires squealed. Julian landed against the tailgate.

"Dude!" he yelled.

Tawd tilted his eyes to the rear-view. Julian was pressed against the back of the truck, arms outstretched, face covered in a t-shirt, and eyes horror stricken.

"I told you to hold on, man" he said, holding back a laugh.

"You're worse than Lisa!" Julian yelled.

Tawd turned to Ed. "How does this guy know Lisa?"

Julian guffawed. "How do I know Lisa? How do you know Lisa? We were together in the Faroes!" He looked at Ed for support.

Ed shrugged.

"Ohhh," Tawd drawled. "You have no idea, do you?"

"What's he talking about?" Julian asked.

"Lisa's the bosun, boy," Tawd snarked. "Means she's the boss."

"You're kidding me."

"Well actually," Ed said. "She's not your boss. You're in the engine room. The chief engineer owns you. Lisa's in charge of all the deck hands." He pointed to Tawd. "Him and about ten others."

"What about you?"

"What about me, what?" Ed held up his hands. "I'm the first mate. You didn't know that either?"

"How would I? And engine room? I'm not an engineer."

The two men burst out laughing.

Tawd glanced into the rear-view. "Better learn quick then, because we're headed out tonight."

Chapter Five: Immersion

It was exactly how he remembered it. The Abbey's white-painted hull cracked under streaks of salted rust. The giant pirate skull glared above the crossed trident and shepherd staff. It was a working ship littered with tools, and hoses, and recovered multi filament nets. Finally, the real deal.

The sun glowered off the water. Julian shielded his eyes.

"You'll get used to that," Ed said. He tossed Julian's bag up the accommodation ladder and scaled the wooden planks onto the ship. Each step clanked off the hull and reverberated across the harbour, joining the cacophony of flapping flags, idling generators, and hammering tools. Julian placed his hands around the coarse webbing and pulled himself up. The ladder heaved as he struggled to place his foot on the first step. Ed made it look so easy. A careful one foot in front of the other and Julian climbed aboard. He picked up his bag and stood observant on the aft-deck.

Compared to the other ships nearby, the Abbey was in pristine condition. Six rusting trawlers were moored to the main wharf. Nets hung in the noonday sun baking the coral, weed, and clinging mud into permanent fixtures. Tires served as fenders, slung over the side of each ship, two at the bow, two at the rear. Seagulls circled above, honing in on the ammonia of the freshly dead fish which were being thrown from one person to the next, all the way up the ramp to the waiting coolers open on the tailgates of the parked trucks.

"Disgusting," Tawd said. He spit over the side of the ship in the direction of the fisherman. "No regard for anything but themselves." He shook his head and disappeared below deck.

Julian shrugged. "It is what it is, I guess."

"It is what it is," Ed agreed. "We better get below, Jules. We're supposed to be heading out tonight."

"Down the hatch it is then."

Ed turned away. "Don't say that."

The mess consisted of three tables and six benches bolted to the floor. Their worn plastic cushions were patched with duct-tape. A stainless steel counter ran the length of one wall separating the mess from the galley. Past that was the dry food storage. The four sun-weathered crew seated at the middle table looked up from their game of cards and waited for Ed to introduce the new volunteer. The cook poked his head out from the galley.

"Julian was with us in the Faroe's," Ed started.

This roused a few nods.

A voice chimed in from the stairwell. "For about two minutes before we ripped cord and retreated off the island, tails tucked between our legs."

Everybody laughed. Julian tried not to blush. He knew the woman's voice before he turned around. He'd recognize Lisa's voice anywhere.

Lisa stood at the top of the stairs, leaning against the bulkhead, smiling.

"It's good to have you on board," she said. Her tone had softened and her light smile made Julian believe she meant it. "Have you met Gilles, yet?"

Julian shook his head.

"Just got down here," Ed said. "On our way to his cabin right now."

Lisa told the card players to shut it down and to come up to prep the deck for cast off. They tossed their cards into a pile at the centre of the table and immediately filed up the stairs. They all seemed eager for action.

Ed led Julian past the food storage then knocked on the open cabin door across. A stringy man spun around in his chair. His long grey horse-tail hair was pulled tight into a pony and hung relaxed under his brimmed camo fishing hat. His deep green eyes, pragmatically still, chilled Julian. Gilles nodded at Ed, who slipped back into the mess, then rubbed his goatee casually.

"You're the new engineer, are you?" he asked.

Julian swallowed. "Yes, sir."

"We'll see," Gilles said matter-of-fact, no malice in his voice.

Julian surveyed the wall above the desk behind where Gilles sat. Leather-bound logs, maintenance textbooks, parts catalogues, and stuffed binders lined the shelf without any apparent order. Business cards with handwritten account numbers and notes were taped to the walls. Oil and fuel filters were crammed in the space between wall and locker. In the corner was a small sink and an angled mirror tilted toward the floor causing anyone who stood in its reflection to appear smaller than lifelike, and if the lighting was just right, as if they'd stepped into a hall of mirrors in an organ whining haunted house. Small engine pieces lay piled in boxes under the sink. A clothesline ran the along the bare wall and had a pair of shorts, a black crew t-shirt, and a pair of swimming trunks hanging from it. The top bunk of the only two beds in the cabin was stripped of its sheets, pillow unsheathed.

"You sleep up there," Gilles said. "Where are your bags?"

Julian thumbed over his shoulder. "Just my backpack," he said.

Gilles smiled. Julian assumed approval.

Ed returned in the doorway. "Um," he said. "I don't really know how to say this, but I think there might be a fire in the engine room."

"A fire?" Gilles asked. "How do you think there might be?"

Julian's face melted. Ed explained. "One of the guys was walking from the aft-cabin and said there were some sparks coming from the generator. Now the mess smells like smoke. Tamara's already had to silence an alarm on the panel. She's in the engine room now."

Gilles rose from his seat, removed a pair of overalls from his locker and slipped into them. He moved unhurried as someone who has routinely operated in emergencies often does. Slow is smooth and smooth is fast. He removed the ear defenders from a hook and placed them on this head. He slid on a pair of safety glasses and told Julian to follow him.

Julian tossed his backpack up on the bunk and trailed after Gilles. They returned through the mess. The space bore a funk of smouldering paint. Several of the crew hung around at the base of the stairway beside the closed door where the smell wafted from. Gilles stepped past them, opened the door, and nodded Julian along. A stack of safety glasses and ear defenders hung neatly above the workbench.

"Put those on," Gilles said. He turned to the hatch opposite the tool room door.

Gilles rolled the hatch-wheel releasing the bars sealing the engine room from the rest of the ship. Exhaust filled the tiny room. Julian hesitated. When Gilles looked back, he still hadn't stepped inside.

"Get in here and shut the door," Gilles said, voice loud enough to be heard over the squealing generator, but not quite yelling. Again, no malice in his voice, simply matter-of-fact.

Julian ducked through the hatch and was greeted by the intense heat of the compartmentalized space. He leaned against the door and used his shoulder to press it shut.

Two engines, the size of mini-vans, towered on either side of the room separated by a narrow gangway leading to a blue panel dotted with gauges, levers, switches, and lights. The starboard generator light flashed red. Julian gripped the gang-rail. He whispered to himself, "I am not and engineer. I am not an engineer. I am not an engineer," as if like Dorthy in the Wizard of Oz, he clicked his heels together he'd be whirled home safe and sound.

Gilles didn't notice or care. He simply pointed to the port side generator; the toy engine compared to the massive ones. Hesitantly, Julian stepped toward it, eyes fixed on Gilles.

A young woman stood poised at the ready beside the smoking generator behind him, hand on the only visible switch, waiting for Gilles' instruction. Julian copied her stature, gripped the cool steel, and waited. Gilles smiled. He pinched his finger and thumb together and twisted his wrist like turning a key in an ignition. Julian pointed to his own hand gripping the switch. Gilles nodded.

Julian turned the switch and let go again. Nothing. Gilles shook his in the negative then imitated turning over a stubborn ignition on a jalopy of a car: wrist cocked in the on position a moment longer. Julian tried again, this time holding the tension a moment longer. The engine rumbled awake sputtering exhaust, then calmed into a rhythmic hum. Gilles spun a dial on the main panel and the needle on the gauge above the generator jumped six-hundred, nine-hundred, fourteen-hundred, and settled on eighteen-hundred revolutions per minute. Later, Julian would learn to never raise the generator's RPM's without first giving it time to warm up– but this was a special circumstance.

Gilles stepped around the control panel, octopus arms up and down and all-over switching switches, dialing dials, and knobbing knobs. When everything appeared satisfactory, Gilles placed a hand on each of the identical levers.

With a resounding crack everything went black. Julian startled. There was another sharp crack and the lights flickered on, the hum of power being drawn from a battery reserve vibrating through the ship's very core. Gilles pointed at the woman on the other generator and sliced the air in front of his throat. She turned the switch and the generator squealed. Even with the ear defenders in place, Julian covered his ears. The panels beneath his feet clamoured. Fight, flight, or freeze–and then silence. Julian exhaled, set his hand on the purring generator, then flinched it away from the heat.

An alarm blared from the control panel. Gilles slapped a button and only the growl of the fresh engine generator remained. Gilles pointed toward the tool room and led the way out. This was how they communicated in the engine room: everything in hands.

The three of them removed their ear defenders, removed their eye protection, and looked at each other. Nobody spoke. Julian shrank in the calm presence of the two who looked exuberant in their accomplishment. Gilles smiled, cool and awkward and chilling.

"Alright," he said. "There's obviously a short somewhere. Probably the last person who had it apart didn't coat one of the connections, came loose and now it's arcing, hence the sparks and smoke." Gilles bore his eyes into the other engineer before staring at Julian, who despite being clueless, wanted to display some semblance of understanding in return. The other engineer nodded so Julian did the same.

"I'm on leave," Gilles said. He looked at his watch, took off his gloves, placed them neatly in the back corner of the tool chest, and stepped toward the mess door. "Starting now. You two let the generator cool. When you get back tonight, maybe in the morning, strip it down, find the loose connection, rubberize it, then bring it back online." Gilles paused. He lifted his chin toward the other engineer. "This is Tamara. She's your third. Once you get acquainted and comfortable, there's a handover on the computer for you. Use that to keep the reports up to date."

Tamara looked at the floor.

"I have a feeling the port generator might have the same issue," Gilles said. "So, once you bring the starboard back on, strip port side and investigate." He placed his hand on the doorknob and turned it. "I'll be back in the fall," he said. "If you have any trouble, radio our sister ship, or send me an email. You'll be alright." Gilles closed the door and the two engineers were alone.

Julian looked the tiny room over. The charts on the walls were covered in grease. The cubbies behind Tamara were littered with hoses and bolts and small engine pieces and tools. Tamara focused her attention on Julian. A smirk came over her face as she realized the new guy was out of his element.

"What did Gilles mean, 'you're my third'?" he asked when he noticed her scrutiny.

Tamara grunted. "Oh," she laughed, but not amused. "Ed didn't tell you that you're acting Chief while Gilles is away?"

"What!"

She shrugged. "Interesting."

"Listen," Julian began. "I didn't ask for this. I don't want it. You've been here longer. I'm happy letting you take the lead."

Tamara shook her head. "Oh no," she said, voice shrill. "You're the boss."

"How can I be in charge? I just got here."

"I'm not staying much longer anyway."

"What are you talking about?" Julian asked. "I thought everybody here were staying at least until May."

"Some even longer," Tamara said. "Just this campaign is different from the last. New captain, won't take risks. We're always in port. The bosun is the biggest, uh, C-U-Next-Tuesday, I've ever met. I don't have a thing about women in charge, feminism, blah, blah, blah, but she's too much."

"Lisa?"

Tamara snapped her eyes and stole a careful look of Julian. "You know her?"

"From the Faroes."

Tamara picked up a socket wrench and a round tote. "So, you know what I'm talking about then." She selected three sockets and placed the tools in the tote. She added a flashlight, two wrenches, a rag, and a small tub of grease. She held the tote to Julian's chest. "No matter what, you're always going to need these tools when you work in there." She thumbed in the direction of the engine room.

He took the tools from her. Julian's mind turned over the thought of Tamara leaving him all by himself.

"You're not even an engineer, are you?" Tamara asked.

"How could you tell?"

"You're not aloof."

They both laughed at that one.

"You don't seem old enough to have your ticket either," Julian joked.

"I wanted in on the action. I did what I had to do to get here, but obviously that was a waste." She slipped on a pair of ear defenders.

"You sound like me in the Faroe's. I was pissed when they called the campaign. I wasn't even there a day. A couple little arrests and everybody fled."

Tamara raised her hands, pouted her lips, and shook her head. She rolled her eyes, pointed to the ear defenders, and showed him her back.

Because she wasn't looking, Julian scrunched his nose and stuck out his tongue at her. When she placed her hands on the large metal wheel, he righted his face. Tamara released the bars which kept the engine room door watertight.

"Come 'on," she hollered, and waved her arm. "I'll show you around."

Julian followed, crouching through the opening, and closed it behind. Tamara stood facing a manifold of yellow pipes and levers. The pipes below the manifold disappeared into the bulkhead; the pipes above ran the length of the room and were fitted with tees which connected the four different engines.

"Fuel!" Tamara yelled. Then she mouthed it.

She pointed to the grey box on the side wall, single black button beside a dim yellow light. "Exhaust!" She exaggerated her mouth like a music teacher emphasizing the tonal scale.

Across the room on the opposite wall hung a similar grey box, black button and adjacent light, only this box wasn't illuminated. Julian raised his hands in question. Tamara leaned in, lifted Julian's ear defender a crack, and shouted, "Only one engine, only one fan! Two or more running get both. You'll kill the crew if you forget."

Tamara winked. Nausea swept Julian. This was not Whale Wars. The fire. Carbon monoxide. Exhaust fans. Dead crew. He was in deep.

The grated steel gangway beneath their feet was divided into three-foot panels. Tamara knelt, slipped her fingers through one of the grates, and lifted the panel from its frame. She clicked the flashlight on and aimed the beam into the hollow. Salt stained and grease dotted pipes, thick as telephone poles, elbowed around the engines and vanished into the hull. Tamara placed the flashlight between her teeth and bit down. She leaned into the floor and placed both hands on the gate-valve's red hand wheel. She turned and turned, arms flexed, until the wheel stopped. Then she gripped one of the triangle levers and cranked it to the left. The triangle tip, the arrow, pointed toward an adjacent pipe. Tamara reached behind her, into the tool bucket, and felt for a spanner-wrench. She slipped the closed end around the t-handle of another valve and cranked it over.

Julian watched, trying to follow each stage, but by now, all the pipes appeared interconnected and the sequence of valves, hand signals, and colours all appeared one oceanic blur.

The floor shifted and the tool bucket slid toward the open grate. Julian grabbed the closest object, the exhaust manifold of the starboard main engine to steady himself. Tamara caught the sliding bucket with her foot, looked up at Julian, and shook her head. She pointed her finger at the manifold Julian had grabbed and wagged her finger back and forth.

"That will burn you when we're at sea!" she yelled.

Julian let go immediately. He raised his arms, motioning he didn't understand.

Tamara waved her hand. "After," she mouthed and resumed her work.

The wheel she'd unscrewed, released a rubber-sealed cover, and exposed the inside of the pipe. A pint-sized stainless-steel screen basket sat snug inside. Tamara removed the basket and set it on the grated floor. Dirt clung to the screen. Seaweed clung to the dirt. Tiny star fish and coral rested on the seaweed.

Tamara pointed to a five-gallon homer bucket stacked near the tool room hatchway, then to the hose coiled on the wall beside it. She pretended to hold the hose in her hand, hand wrapped around vacant air, and pointed the imaginary spout over the invisible tool bucket. "Water," she mouthed.

Finally, Julian thought, something he could do.

Julian filled the bucket and set it beside Tamara, who dunked the screen basket into it and brushed away all the debris. Like clenching a fist, the little starfish puckered into tight balls. Tamara returned the basket to the pipe, ran a bead of grease-oil over the rubber seal, and tightened it closed. She pointed to the red hand wheel, stood up, and nodded for Julian to get down and turn it himself.

Julian set his hands to the greasy wheel, immediately released his grip, and wiped his hands on his pants.

Tamara laughed. She spun her finger in a circle and stared at the wheel.

Julian resumed his position and cranked the hand wheel until it stopped.

When Julian looked up, Tamara was pointing at the grate. Julian nodded. She picked up the homer bucket full of water, turned, and opened the hatch to the tool room.

Julian positioned the grate, retrieved the tools and followed Tamara out of the engine room. When he'd closed the hatch behind him, he turned to find Tamara waiting, holding a white pamphlet to her chest. For a moment, Julian paused, noticing for the first time, her independent beauty. She'd removed her ball cap and allowed her auburn hair, bangs trimmed straight and sidelong to her shoulders, to hang free. Traces of pink streaked from root to end in tasteful rebellion. Though she wasn't smiling, Julian imagined shy dimples and teeth lightly exposed.

"Oi!" She snapped her fingers. Her eyes narrowed with the tilt of her head. "Don't get all googly-eyes with me."

He blushed and stuttered something unintelligible.

"I'm just messing with you," she said. She raised the pamphlet in front of his face.

"What's this?" Julian asked, regaining his composure.

"The most important thing you'll learn on this campaign." She set the pamphlet on the tool chest. "First, let's talk about in there." She pointed to the engine room door. "Those are the biggest pipes on the ship," she said. "Biggest." She stared. The ominous words hung on Julian's ears. "Means, if when the engines are running and the water is pumping, if you forget to close the hand wheel–" She paused, picked up the pamphlet, and revealed the title. "You're going to sink the ship."

The cover was a crude illustration of a sinking ship and a smiling whale. At the top it read: How to Sink a Ship.

"You're going to read this, memorize as much as you can, and give it back."

Julian nodded.

"If this ever left the shift, if the public ever found out this was still our mandate, we'd lose all sorts of funding."

"I thought you said we don't do this type of thing anymore," Julian said. "That the reason you're leaving campaign is that nobody is doing anything anymore."

Tamara sucked her lips. "A few of us still believe." She handed the pamphlet over. "You know what? Don't even take it from this room. Not all the crew would be on board either." She started to hang the tools on their Sharpie-silhouetted positions. "Those pipes we were working on. Those are the salt-water intakes. Basically, what you're going to read is: open the basket seat, ditch the lid, open the valve, and get off the ship. Quick-time."

The radio crackled. "Engineer, engineer, engineer."

Tamara pulled the device from her pocket and pressed it to her lips. "This is Engineer, over."

"Get those engines started," the woman's voice commanded. "We're Oscar Mike in ten."

She replied, "Roger, over," then returned the radio to her pocket. "No matter how many times we've told her, she always waits until the last second to fire up the engines," Tamara said. "They won't even be warm in ten minutes and the first thing she's going to do outside the break wall is throw down the accelerator and—" She grabbed her ear defenders. "Forget it. Come on. I'll show you how to fire these things up."

Julian set the pamphlet on the tool bin, grabbed his own ear defenders and trailed after Tamara.

"It's really complicated," Tamara yelled over the purring generator.

She stood in front of the panel at the end of the gangway. The top section were lights labelled with their corresponding parts: generator, oil pressure, RPM, fuel, and a dozen other terms Julian didn't recognize. Below the lights were gauges, and below the gauges were push buttons, each inscribed with their own action: port engine, starboard engine, override, reset.

Tamara placed a finger on the Port engine push button and another on the Reset. She pressed the engine button. The room shook. The alarm light, Low Engine Pressure, screamed at the top of the panel. Tamara pressed the reset button. The alarm stopped, though the light remained illuminated red.

Tamara moved her hands to the Starboard side of the panel, positioned her fingers like she had on the Port side, and pressed the Engine to start. Another alarm blared, which Tamara silenced, before moving to inspect the physical gauges on the engines themselves. The needles noted the rising pressure. Tamara pointed to the highlighted areas on each gauge, where the needles had not yet climbed, and gave the thumbs up. There was no chance of being heard with both engines roaring. Julian remembered the exhaust fans and nodded toward the box that wasn't lit up. Tamara nodded. Julian hurried over and turned on the fan.

Next she pointed to the hatch-wheel. Julian spun it unlocked. He pulled on the handle, but the door wouldn't budge. He looked at Tamara, who laughed. Tamara gripped the handle with both hands and yanked it toward her. The door swung open.

Inside the tool room, Julian struggled to pull the hatch shut. When he finally had, Tamara was leaned up against the task board, still giggling.

"That's some crazy suction," Julian said, eyes popped.

"You're going to have a good laugh watching any of the crew do that. They trip every time."

"I thought you said turning the engines on was complicated," Julian said.

"I thought I told you not to leave this lying around." She picked up the 'How to Sink a Ship' booklet off of the tool chest. Julian sucked his lips and half shrugged.

"Engineer, engineer, engineer."

Tamara removed a radio from the charger and told the captain they would be ready to cast off in ten. She handed it to Julian. "Clip the tether to your belt, keep it on channel eight, and leave it in your pocket. You'll only need to answer if I don't, unless it's your shift. Basically, every response is, 'Yes,' or 'I'm on it.'"

"Okay," Julian said. "But what if the answer is no, or I don't have the answer?"

"It's never no or I can't. You're an engineer now, Chief. You can do anything. And if you can't, make it up. It's easy."

Julian wasn't convinced.

"Let's go topside and watch the horror show. These guys are terrible at casting off."

Chapter Six: Acquisition

All the crew who were playing cards in the mess, and a few Julian hadn't met yet, stood on the starboard side of the Edward Abbey holding thick braided ropes in their hands. Tawd stood on the floating dock that the ship was moored to. Lisa paced the deck, inspecting the ropes and each of the crew's positions. She spoke into her radio, listened, and responded. Nothing came though on Julian's radio, or Tamara's.

"Deck crew uses a different channel," Tamara said as if reading his mind. She clicked over a couple digits. The captain was confirming details with Lisa. "See."

All of a sudden, she started patting his arm excitedly. "Keep your eyes on Rodriguez back there." Tamara pointed to the round Mexican standing above a cleat. "He nearly falls in the drink every time."

The captain radioed the engineers, Tamara confirmed the engines were ready, and the ship shifted forward, tugging at the dock. The engines then returned to idle. Tawd released the bow line, about-turned, and ran back to release the spring line. The deck crew pulled the ropes in as fast as they could. A team near the front tripped over each other, but they continued to retrieve from where they fell on the deck. Lisa radioed something to the captain, and the boat lurched into reverse, guided by the remaining stern line and angled toward the harbour's entrance. When the line slackened, Tawd released it, and Rodriguez leaned over the life lines to retrieve the rope.

"I don't think it's going to happen this time," Tamara said, disappointment in her voice.

The rope piled up behind Rodriguez. Lisa updated the captain and the boat jerked forward. Rodriguez lost his balance. He stepped on the pile of stern line and hit the deck hard.

Tamara doubled over. "Every time!" she said. "Every time! It's the best part of my day."

Rodriguez righted himself against the life lines and sheepishly scanned the deck to make sure no-one had seen his blunder. Tamara waved and yelled, "Love you, Rody!"

Rodriguez grunted, kicked the pile of rope, and sulked toward the aft-cabin hatch. Lisa appeared from the side of the ship. "I don't think so," she said, hands pressed to her hips in a comically tyrannical posture; as all tyrants are laughable in their most serious of moments. "Do you want that happening to someone else? Coil the rope," she said. "You know better than that."

Rodriguez slapped his arms by his side, hung his head, and huffed as he knelt beside the pile.

Julian curbed his smile as he watched Rodriguez scowl his way through the task. "Animated little fella', isn't he?"

Tawd waved goodbye to the ship from where he stood on the dock.

"What about Tawd?" he asked.

"He'll take the panga and meet us outside the break wall."

Tamara fiddled with her radio to make sure she was on the engineer channel before slipping it back into her pocket. She looked up to see Julian bobbing his head, nodding along pretending to understand, but his eyes betrayed his confusion.

"The panga is that bass boat at the end of the dock, only we don't call it a bass boat because fishermen are literally the Nazi's of the sea." Tamara winked.

If Julian was confused a moment ago, he was swimming now, unsure if she was seriously invoke the Third Reich or only pulling his leg. Nazi's?

The Abbey steered the calm water of the harbour, cleared the break wall, and began to drift with the guiding swell. The ship rolled side over side, a feeling Julian had only ever experienced once before, drunk at his parent's anniversary, the night he clung disoriented to the toilet in the women's bathroom and vomited red bile until he passed out. The unstable footing he never wanted to experience again, and hadn't, one of those lucky ones whose first collision with the mistress bottle turned him tee-total by first light. Instantly his stomach churned.

"Up here you feel it more, but you'll get used to it," Tamara said. "Do you want me to rub your belly?" She reached for Julian's stomach only to have her hand swatted away.

"I just need to get my sea legs," Julian said. "I'll be fine." He gripped the fly deck's railing.

"Watch the water and don't resist the roll," Tamara said. "Ride it."

Julian thought about the heat of the engine room, the enclosed space, and the little swell that threatened the tool bucket into the open floor panel. How he grabbed the closest steady object, which happened to be the exhaust manifold of the starboard engine, and how if it had been running, he would have scolded his arms.

"You're not looking out to sea," Tamara said, deadpan. "I'm not taking you under until you get a handle on this. If you throw up in engine room, gawd, Gilles will never let you hear the end of it. It would be like you spewed all over his baby's face."

Julian raised his gaze from his feet and over the side of the ship. The water moved in colour. The darkest hues slopped against the Abbey's hull and returned toward the horizon, softening into mulberry and mauve and pearl in the sunset. He inhaled. Slowly his stomach-storm abated. Julian stared into the horizon and realized all he could see was water. No shoreline, no islands, only sea. He expected panic to arise, first time farther than he could comfortably swim and easily overwhelmed by the ocean's vastness, but it never came.

"There you go," Tamara said. She patted Julian's back. "My favourite part of this job is coming up here and looking beyond. It's about claiming the little things while you can, you know?"

Tamara faced the stern. Rodriguez finished coiling the rope and was climbing into the aft-cabin hatch to hide awhile. Out of the marina harbour, a small boat led a trail of white toward the Abbey. She rested her hands on the railing and stared into the distance.

"The little things," she said. "Because stuff happens out here that you could never predict."

A shrill whiz like a dentist drill shot into the air above the bridge. Julian cocked his head to follow the sound into the sky.

"I can't believe they're sending them out with the weather coming in like it is," Tamara said.

Julian cupped his eyes. The black device hovered, tilted, then sped out to sea. He followed the drone until it became a singular blinking light.

"They're like thirty-grand a piece," she continued. "And we've already lost two on this campaign—both times in an approaching storm!" Tamara washed her hands together and shook them in the direction of the drone.

"Whatever," she whined, her adolescent twang fully audible. "Not my problem."

"What are they looking for?" Julian asked.

"Investigating blips on the radar, probably," she said. "But they just love flying the things, so it could very well be nothing."

"I hope it's something," Julian said.

The Abbey rolled with the increasing swells and a crash came from inside the bridge.

"I hope we turn around and wait until calmer waters," Tamara said, shaking her head. "I better go investigate whatever just fell. It'll probably end up being some new engineer task." She stepped down the ladder and slipped into the bridge.

"Give me a hand!" a man's voice yelled from below. Tawd had manoeuvred the panga to the side of the Abbey, but there were no crew to greet him. "Come on!" He hollered. The swell butted the panga against the Abbey with a thundering gong.

Julian jumped the ladder and ran down the stairs. He stood ready at the life lines above the panga. Tawd's face was wild. He waved a carabiner above his head. "I'm going to throw you the painter line. Clip it to the stanchion, then I'll board and show you how to bring this thing into tow."

"Ready!" Julian boomed, surprising himself. But he wasn't ready. The ship rolled as Tawd threw the line and instead of catching it, Julian grabbed a stanchion and the carabiner tied to the end of the painter disappeared into the dark waters. Tawd scrambled to retrieve the line into the panga. Hand over hand, he pulled until he reclaimed the sopping carabiner.

Tawd gritted his teeth. "Again."

Julian leaned over the lines and caught it this time. He clipped it to the stanchion and waited.

Tawd didn't speak. He scaled the accommodation ladder and glared at Julian.

Julian readied himself for the punch he thought was coming.

"Bridge, bridge, drone team," Tawd's radio crackled.

"Bridge," the captain said.

"We have a visual on the target, over."

"Confirm the target is illegal."

A light static buzzed over the receiver. "Target is illegal, over."

Tamara poked her head out of the bridge hatch, waving a pair of binoculars.

"Come see this," Tamara said.

Julian's relief pooled into a smile. He shrugged at Tawd, scooted around him, and ran up the steps.

Tamara handed him the binos. "You can follow the green light to where the drone is hovering. Right below are the poachers."

Julian squinted through the lenses and honed in on the location. It was too tiny a boat to be out on the rough waters. The high bow and narrow waterline beam, same as the one Tawd planed in on, made the panga unmistakable. White hull, light blue interior contrasted by the yellow and orange waders that the five-man crew wore made them impossible to miss against the darkening blue water. The two-hundred horsepower motor mounted to the transom looked very wrong.

"They'll blow themselves out of the water," Julian said.

Lisa appeared in the companionway. "Do you want a crew for the panga?"

"No," the captain said.

Tamara leaned in. "We can't pursue at speed if we're towing."

The captain rubbed her face. She looked toward the deck and didn't speak. One of the drone crew stood against the windlass with his arms stretched above his head in a V. The drone hovered above his hands, blades whirling in a blur. He reached for the skids. When both hands gripped tight, the drone operator cut the engines, and the blades stopped spinning. They placed the drone into the hard Pelican case and looked up to the captain. She waved, 'come here,' then addressed Lisa.

"It's too rough to put our crew out there," she said, then turned to Tamara. "Why can't we haul it up with the crane and set it on the cradle?"

Tamara scratched her chin. "It's too rough."

"Send Ben and someone else back to the harbour then," she told Lisa. "They can go up to the house and wait until we come in."

Lisa hesitated then retreated down the companionway.

"It's all we can do," Tamara offered.

"Better ready the crew," the captain said.

She flicked the red plastic cover beside the ships internal communication line. It revealed a silver toggle switch. The captain clicked the switch over. Immediately, a leisurely wail wound up through the speakers before speeding into a loud siren. It reminded Julian of the long whine of a fire station releasing their fleet of firetrucks.

Tamara signalled for Julian to follow her out.

Crew scurried from the mess and into their cabins to retrieve their life vests. Hatches opened and closed. People cursed as they tripped over the large steps through each sealed division of the ship. Tamara and Julian tucked themselves into the tool room and turned one of their radios to the bosun's channel.

"Panga crew is detached from the ship and en route to the harbour." Lisa's voice reported.

"Copy that," the captain said. "En route to the target."

There was a pause. The captain then spoke over engineer's channel.

"Engineer, this is Bridge. Are we good to pursue at speed?"

Tamara pressed the petzel switch and spoke into the receiver. "Engineer, we are ready."

She clipped the radio to her pocket and pulled her ear defenders snug on her ears. Julian copied and spun the engine room hatch wheel open. They stopped in front of the engine gauges.

Tamara tapped the RPM and hollered, "Watch her jump this."

The engines growled as they revved from idle to fifteen hundred revolutions per minute. The bow rose out of the water and the propellers whirled into action. Julian steadied himself. The floor panels shook. Tamara seemed unaffected. She turned around and focused on the opposite gauges' panel. After a moment, they retreated to the tool room.

Julian gasped as he struggled to close the hatch behind him.

"You weren't kidding about the noise," Julian said. "Or the strength of the suction." He wiped his hands on his shirt.

"You'll get used to it quick enough. The engine roar will soften," Tamara said. "Or you'll start to go deaf."

"...five minutes," the radio warned. "I want the spotlight tracking and cameras rolling the entire time. Five minutes," the captain repeated. "We'll have them in range in five minutes."

The alarm had stopped blaring. The engine's growl tore through the ship.

"Let's go topside and see if we can't glimpse the action," Tamara said.

Chapter Seven: Overboard

"There are four of them on board," the captain said.

Tamara perched herself in the first mate's seat. Julian leaned on the chart table behind her.

"Are they running yet?" Tamara asked.

"I think they're about to cut the net and make a go for it."

The captain confirmed with the media crew that the cameras were live and the spotters were ready to engage the floodlight. Because the bridge opened up to the fly deck it was a natural perch to liaison all that conspired in the war room and the effects of those discourses on the water around the Edward Abbey.

Tamara hung her head. "This is the worst time of day for this," she whispered. "Dusk. Already the swell. They're in a panga for gods-sake." She raised her gaze and held the binos to her eyes. Four poachers. And just like the captain anticipated, two of the men were cutting the net free. The man seated behind the steering wheel scrambled with the fuel lines to prime the engine. He squeezed the palm-sized football lung several times before adjusting the choke and getting ready on the rip cord. The smaller poacher on the bow wore a red baseball cap and a white face mask. He looked out of place, if for size alone, his almost youthful innocence haloed over the backdrop of all seriousness. Everybody's heads were down.

The panga's engine squealed as the boat shot out of the water, over the swell, and left a trail of turbulent white in its wake.

"They're on the move," the spotters reported through the open bridge door below.

Tamara covered her mouth muttering what Julian thought might be: "Don't give suit. Don't give suit…" But could have been a prayer of some sort. Or nothing.

The captain commanded pursuit. Tamara's eyes remained glued to the four poachers bouncing in their panga.

"They're at thirty knots," someone said.

Tamara gasped and dropped the binoculars. A large white splash exploded behind the panga. "One of them is in the water!" she cried.

"Spotter, this is Bridge," the captain said. "Do we have a man overboard out there?"

The silence hung heavy over the radio.

Julian followed the beam of light as it scanned the dark waters.

"Negative," the spotters said.

"I swear to God," Tamara said. "Someone fell in."

The captain hesitated then pulled back on the accelerator and brought the ship's engines to a drifting six-hundred revolutions per minute idle.

"They're all in orange, yellow, and red," Tamara said, eyes firm against the binocular lenses. "He won't be hard to find."

"Bridge," the radio crackled.

The captain returned the call.

"Uh," the reluctant voice started. "We have a man overboard, two o'clock, 500 metres ahead."

The Bridge stared in that direction.

Julian was first to get eyes on. "There," he said, arm reaching starboard, two o'clock.

The captain picked up the UHF. "Navy Two, Navy Two, this is the Edward Abbey, over."

Navy Two responded, "Go ahead."

"We put the spotlight onto a small fishing boat at our current location," the captain reported. "The fishing boat fled with speed and crashed. There is a man overboard and we are moving ahead to recover him."

"Do you want us to come and assist?" Navy Two asked.

"Negative," the captain said. "We have the spotlight on him and life rings ready, over."

"We are on standby," Navy Two replied.

The captain set down the handset and sighed. She took the binos from Tamara and scanned the water. One lone individual dressed in orange waders and yellow jacket, hands reaching ghostly toward the Abbey, bobbed in the foreboding water.

The sun had disappeared during the excitement. The captain rested the binos and flicked on all the exterior lights. The stalled panga drifted silently on the starboard side. Its two crew stood mouths agape, hands resting on their hips, and stared.

"They might have blown their engine," Tamara said.

The captain didn't acknowledge.

Below, on the bow, Lisa organized her crew into recovery teams. She positioned them several metres apart, staggered along the lifelines, in the same positions they assume when casting off. This time, however, in each team one person held a life ring and the other the life ring's coiled rope.

Lisa spoke into her radio: "We are throwing the life rings now." She pointed her hand at the team in the middle, then tapped the team closest to where she stood on the bow. The two teams heaved their life rings in tandem, then watched, waiting for the poacher to reach for one of them.

"Just grab it," the captain said–to nobody, to herself, to the drowning man. "We're going to need a medic when we get him on board," she said, also ambiguously directed.

Tamara reached for the radio, assuming she expected her to make the call. The captain shook her head no, picked up the handset, and asked Navy Two to send medical assistance.

The man in the water reached one of the life rings. Rodriguez yelled at him to slip into it but the man wouldn't or couldn't; he just hung on. Lisa distributed the extraction poles, the kind lifeguards use with a large wire scoop at one end. The teams took turns trying to hook the ring, or the line, or the man, in order to pull him toward the Abbey.

Tawd hooked him. "I'm on!" he yelled.

Lisa hung the pilot ladder over the side of the ship and waited for Tawd and his partner to pull him in.

Up close, the man's face was not the face of a hardened poacher. He was just a boy, not more than sixteen years old. If he was panicked, he didn't appear so. In fact, his body limped. Rodriguez ordered him to climb the ladder. If the ship rolled, he'd surely go under with it. The boy grabbed the first slat. When he attempted to lift himself, he slumped back into the sea. Each attempt submersed him all over again.

"This isn't going to work," Ed told Lisa. "I'm going to fire up the crane."

He removed the straps which secured the boom to the deck, then pressed the power button. The crane whined. One of the crew complained that Ed wasn't wearing his safety helmet. Tawd smacked the back of his head. "Don't be an idiot."

The crane reached beyond the side of the ship and waited its next manipulation. Lisa leaned over the life lines, eyes trained on the boy in the water, and waved her hand in a circle above her head. Ed pulled a lever, and the cable lowered. She cupped her hands around her mouth and yelled something at the boy. He gazed through her, aloof in his condition. She grabbed the cable and shook it violently. The boy jerked his head, recognition flooding into his eyes, and he reached for the cable. Rodriguez told him to pull the sling over his body. When the boy had, Lisa signalled above her head, Ed pushed on the lever, and the cable tightened, slowly lifting its load out of the water. He positioned the boom over the aft-deck and lowered the boy. Tawd and Ed freed him from the sling and helped him below into the mess, the predesignated emergency medical station.

The wait dragged on for what felt like hours before the first report made its way to the bridge.

"Possible hypothermia," the voice on the radio crackled. It was Ed. "Send me Rodriguez," he continued. "I can't understand a word this kid is saying."

"Why is Ed doing the medical stuff," Julian asked. "I thought he was first mate."

"He wears a lot of hats," Tamara said.

The captain told Julian to fetch Rodriguez and to bring him below. Julian jumped up, was out the rear hatch, and running down the stairs before she finished her command.

He brought Rodriguez to the mess and both of them helped the medic strip the boy from his waterlogged clothes. The cook boiled water for a hot drink.

"Find out what he's jabbering about," Ed said to Rodriguez, then set to work fitting his patient with a blood pressure cuff, a heart monitor, and a thermometre. Julian wrapped him in emergency blankets.

Rodriguez and the poacher spoke in rapid succession. After a flurry of incoherent rambling, Rodriguez turned to Ed and said, "I think there's someone else in the water."

"What?"

"He keeps telling me, 'Please, my brother, my little brother is gone under.'"

Everybody stared at the boy. He didn't speak, only nodded his head over and over.

Ed picked up the radio and called the captain.

The deck crew had begun stowing the life rings, returning the poles, and re-rolling the pilot ladder to be tucked away. When the last item was stowed, the slow hi-low wail of the emergency sirens screamed back to life. The crew looked up in bewilderment. The captain emerged from the passage and yelled for all eyes on the water.

"There's another person out there," she said. "The navy is on their way." She turned to reenter the bridge, paused, then said, "The search ends when we find him."

Lisa called the captain on her radio to confirm what needed to be done. She nodded to her crew. "You heard the captain. Same teams when we were doing the recovery, all eyes out there."

"I'm going back to the deck," Tawd said, not looking at anyone. He shook his head and muttered something under his breath as he ascended the stairs.

The cook emerged from the galley with a steaming mug. A hint of peppermint trailed him, rising to fill the cabin. The calming scent slowly began to massage the tension smothering the minds of all those present in the mess. He set the mug in front of the boy. The steam fogged the dull reflection of the tinfoil emergency blanket wrapped around the boy. Instead of accepting the offering, the boy's hands remained rested in his lap.

Bright white scars marred his open palms. He had callouses the size of quarters beneath each finger.

"Mi hermano, mi hermano," the boy repeated, tranced. "Mi hermano."

The cook rested his hand on the boy's shoulder. "Estará bien, encontraremos a tu hermano."

Julian and Rodriguez cocked their heads at the cook, the German. Neither of them knew he could speak Spanish. The young boy lifted his distant stare and met eyes with the cook. He nodded his head. "Gracias." It's then he reached for the mug. The cook nodded then returned to the galley.

Topside, Lisa's shivering deck teams scanned the water. Their adrenaline from the first rescue had worn off and the cool after-storm air of the sea had settled around them. The bridge managed the spot lights and used them to run Z-patterns over the surface of the black water. One light aimed port side, the other aimed over the starboard side. Each traced fifty-metre squares, then zagged up and down the area in between. The radios remained mute. Nobody spoke. At least nobody transmitted.

Leaned against a stanchion, chinned raised and head titled back in disapproval, Tawd continued his stammering only now he didn't restrain himself. "If we haven't found the little spic by now," he said, letting the sentiment hover its mortality. Tawd dropped the life ring on the deck and jerked the line away from his partner.

"But we're supposed to be ready to throw those."

Tawd glared at him. He tossed the line on top of the life ring at his feet. "Consider it thrown."

"Whatever," he said, unwilling to engage Tawd's predilection. He returned his attention to the sea and continued scanning the arcs that Lisa had assigned him.

"You're not really trying to find him, are you?" Tawd leaned against the bulkhead. He picked at his dreads like a baboon inspecting for lice. "They're poachers. Scum of the earth. They're the reason we're out here.

They're the reason we keep turning up dead dolphins. All those totoaba. That sperm whale last week. Remember that?"

Tawd stuck out his tongue and pretended to gag. "All those seagulls gawking and crapping over its bloated carcass. Same poachers." He hawked a loogie over the side of the ship. "I hope the kid's drowned. It would serve them right."

"I hope you never say that with the cameras around," the voice from behind reprimanded.

Tawd snapped to standing. He hadn't noticed Lisa in the companion way. "We're out here to save lives," Lisa continued. She stepped in front of Tawd and picked up the life line and ring. "I don't care if it's all the children in Mexico, or the remaining Vaquita: I'm here to save lives." She pressed the ring to Tawd's chest and stared. Tawd limply accepted. "Now do your job and scan the waters." Lisa picked up her radio and called the bridge. "Bridge this is bosun."

"Go ahead, bosun," came the crackled response.

"Do you have any updates from Navy Two? We don't have eyes on anything down here."

"Navy Two is still en route to claim the first boy."

Lisa focused on Tawd. He glared at the sea with a clenched jaw.

"All this anger you have," she said. "It's a little irrational, don't you think? I mean, we're animals, too." She bit her lip. "Seems to me you're acting like a self-hating Jew."

Tawd launched the life ring across the deck. It smashed into the fire box. A deep, weighted thud reverberated across the ship. The teams startled before composing themselves, trying to ignore the situation. He started to hyperventilate and finally managed: "That's...that's...that's...ra-cist!"

Lisa threw her arms up. "And you calling the missing boy a spic wasn't?"

"You're making light of the massacre of an entire race of people," Tawd snarled. "That boy you're referring to, that–" he swallowed a pause. He choked his Adam's apple for added effect. "That murderer–" he said in heavy condemnation. He bore holes into Lisa with his lunatic stare.

"That boy? These people are destroying our oceans. Everyday they're creating their own holocaust. And for what? Money? Profit? I'd sooner drown the entire lot of them if it would save one animal life. These defenceless dolphins are just trying to survive."

The wind picked up in a gust and tested the ship's flag lines which clanged against the mast. Lisa frowned. Tawd's partner continued his scan, face blank, pretending not to listen.

"I for one will not turn a blind eye to the horror," Tawd continued. "All it takes for evil to prevail is for good people to do nothing!"

Lisa retrieved the life ring. She held it at her hip. "Go inside," she said stoically. She handed the life ring to Tawd's partner and assumed Tawd's post. "I can't look at you right now." She shook her head. "That's somebody's kid out there. Somebody's brother. And yeah, our mandate is ocean conservation, but where's your humanity?" Lisa looked over her shoulder toward Tawd. "I'm serious. Go inside. You're done here."

Tawd rolled spittle on his tongue and spat it over the side.

"And just so we're perfectly clear," Lisa added. "When this is all said and done and we're back in the harbour, I'm recommending the captain remove you from our campaign. I don't want you on my crew. Now go."

This last bit was like splashing water on a Gremlin. Tawd's smirk grew. He seemed to tower where he stood. He bit his tongue and curbed his eye brows. "Good luck." He winked. "I'm more Legion than you'll ever be. Friggin' fire me! Ha! That's a joke. I'll probably get your job for my stance on the issue." Tawd clicked his heels together and straightened up. He snapped his open palm to his forehead in a mock salute daring Lisa. Then with all the disrespect of a disgruntled soldier forced to play the subservient part, he jerked his arm to his side and marched fists swinging breast pocket high into the companionway. His final act, to ice his grand exit, when out of sight but not out of earshot, he scoffed, "Nazi sympathizer."

Lisa shook her head. She wiped the base of her eyes then cupped her hands over her lips. In through the nose out through the mouth, she breathed.

"Uh, Lisa," a timid voice hesitated.

She shook from her wondering.

It was Tawd's partner. "I think I have eyes on," he continued, pointing to sea.

Lisa followed the trajectory of his outstretched hand.

Floating with the swell, not a hundred feet away, a dull orange shadow rose and fell without resistance.

Lisa radioed the bridge for spotlight support. On the other side of the ship, port side, the navy RIB was tying on.

"We see what you see," the bridge reported.

The deck crew held their collective breath. Even the wind stopped blowing.

"Navy Two will investigate."

The RIB's engines whined as the boat manoeuvred around the bow of the Abbey and crept toward the floating orange object.

A second RIB arrived and tied up to the ship. Several of their crew boarded, skipped the steps up to the bridge, and vanished inside. The captain called for Ed to bring the rescued boy topside. The navy would take him to shore for further medical treatment.

In the distance, the first navy RIB cut its engines and began drifting beside the floating mark. The men stood abreast, hands linked behind their heads, staring into the water. The radio remained silent.

Lisa turned from her post and hung the life ring on its rack. "It's the boy."

One-by-one, the teams turned from their positions and replaced their life rings.

"Everybody head inside," Lisa said. "Get some hot fluids into you. Change your clothes. It's been a long day. You all did well." She leaned against a stanchion then looked back toward the navy boat. "We'll debrief at dinner."

The crew slowly shuffled into the ship without a word. Across the water, leaning into the swell, the four men pulled at the boy, trying to haul him aboard. The last thing Lisa saw before following her crew below was the splayed child, arm and leg being pulled over the side of the RIB, his other arm and leg reaching, not yet ready to let go of the sea.

Chapter Eight: Campaign

The first page read, "The Trident Legion exists for one purpose: To defend, conserve and protect the seas and marine wildlife at all costs."

Julian set the Edward Abbey's Rules of Engagement binder on his desk and let go a deep sigh. There were thirty more pages to get through, then all the ship's manuals, and then all the ship's logs. Already his brain was awash.

He leaned back in his chair, tilted the binder over the edge of the desk, and skimmed the rest of the page. The Legion's claim to be the largest private navy on the planet drew his attention, but the rest of the script he already knew. The Legion positioned themselves on the front lines to expose the truth; the Legion risked the lives of their crew to save marine wildlife; the Legion operated in contentious waters to war with poachers and other illegal outfits. The Legion was a law unto itself, above the law, for they operated on principle.

After the day's events, it all read like propaganda.

Propaganda. Propaganda. Propaganda.

The chapter concluded with Captain Saul Swatson's siren call. Julian used a booming voice to read it out loud. "Unless we stop the degradation of our oceans, marine ecological systems will begin collapsing. When enough of them fail the oceans will die." He paused. "And if the oceans die, then we all die."

Chapter Nine: Retrieval

A month had passed since the young man had drowned on that choppy February eve in the Sea of Cortez. The Abbey crew had settled into a routine and were busy retrieving abandoned nets. The mission was simple enough: The ship and its crew were to patrol the waters in and around the gill net exclusion zone, an overlay on the map that prohibited fishing in a government sanctioned effort to protect the timid and cute Vaquita marina dolphin from total extinction.

The engineers kept the engines running on their massive reservoir of diesel fuel while the deck crew trolled for gill nets: the ones deployed by poachers in an active pursuit of the totoaba, and the gill nets forgotten and left to rot by the fishermen of old. The longer the nets stayed submerged, the greater the body count of all the fishes and mammals who call home the sea.

Some nets came up clean, but this was rare. Most retrievals involved untangling the animals that were trapped but still alive, documenting their particulars, and releasing them back into the water. If the animals came up dead, however, the process was the same, only sombre.

"I'm heading up," Julian said. He hung his gear in the tool crib. "Sounds like they have a big one on their hands."

Tamara shook her head. "There's no way I'm topside if they're pulling in a bunch of dead fish." She stuck out her tongue and pretended to choke. "That smell gets in my hair and it lingers for weeks. I have nightmares falling asleep it's so bad."

"I don't know why they don't just keep all the fish they catch. I mean, there's enough there to feed a village for months."

Tamara didn't even try to disguise the disbelief which stole over her face. "Give the fish to the people who are littering these nets all over the ocean? To the only known predators hurrying along the Vaquita holocaust? 'Hey guys, I know we're sworn enemies and all, but we stumbled over one of your nets, retrieved it for you, and hey, here's your catch.'" She nipped her eyes. "Not to mention we're vegan, remember? Or did you forget that, too?"

"Well, that's something that doesn't make sense to me either."

Tamara half-rolled her eyes and allowed her mouth to lop open in utter annoyance.

"You can't tell me Captain Saul Swatson is vegan, he's like three-hundred pounds—our commander and chief, the Legion's founder for god's sake—where's the consistency of image there?"

Tamara's annoyance was quickly becoming rabid. "Did you just fat shame Captain Swatson?"

Julian tossed his dirty rag into the used rag bucket. "It's messed up."

"It's something alright," Tamara said as she tinkered with what looked like small engine pieces. "I wouldn't share those thoughts outside this room, you know? I'm one thing. Us engineers gotta stick together and all. But the rest of the crew—"

"What are you doing here anyway?" Julian asked. He waved his hand over the scattered mess.

Tamara continued to dig through the crate of miscellaneous parts. Occasionally she'd remove something and add it to the collection on the floor. "I want to get that Honda water pump working again." She held up a rubber impeller, inspected it, and placed it among the other pieces. "The last people that used it didn't rinse it out after. Now it's all corroded and seized up."

"Sounds like a make-work project to me," Julian said. "I'll be up watching from the fly deck to make sure the captain doesn't prop foul us in the net."

Tamara chuckled, but didn't look up from her task. "I'll see you down here in twenty then. Shot-not diving to cut us free when she does."

They guffawed over their insider engineer joke. In the month of patrolling, at the very least twice a week, whenever the Abbey had hooked onto a net and the crew began retrieving, the captain, somehow, always managed to reverse the ship into the submerged portion and entangle the propeller. They'd have to cut nets free. Someone, either one of the two engineers, would have to gear up in S.C.U.B.A., and dive below to saw through the braids of line that were wound tight around the shaft arresting the propeller.

Julian straightened his face. "If she fouls again, I'm done. I'm terrified to dive down there." And he was serious. Stories of the captain ordering the engines turned on when divers were under on previous campaigns tortured him whenever he suited up to investigate a prop foul.

Thumb up, Tamara clicked her tongue. "Here's hoping."

Topside, Lisa had her crew readied on the fore deck. A large yellow buoy bobbed beside the Abbey. Tawd leaned over the stanchion line. He held a grappling hook tethered to a black braided rope.

"Go for it," Lisa said.

He reached his hand behind his head, flicked his wrist around twice, and pitched the welded rebar toward the buoy. It sunk behind the target. Tawd slowly began stringing it in. The rope tightened. He grinned at Rodriguez. "That's why you're on the windlass and I'm up here. First try every time."

Rodriguez flipped him the bird. "Everybody is so-ooo impressed, Tawd."

The bridge interrupted. "You're going to have to let it go." The crew cocked their heads toward the glowering windows of the bridge. The captain pointed. "We're drifting toward the net and need to correct before we get into trouble."

Like a child gloating, Rodriguez stuck out his tongue and wagged it at Tawd. "Guess it's not first try after all."

"That's crap," Tawd scoffed. "She's got to get better control of the ship. We never used to have these issues." He released his grip and allowed the line to slip into the sea. In a few seconds, all which remained of the net were a few yellow football-sized floats bobbing on the surface. Tawd shook his head disgustedly. "I don't know why Ed just doesn't take the controls. This never happens when he's in command."

The ship lurched into reverse, destabilizing the crew. Nobody fell, but everybody definitely wobbled some. When the captain squared the ship to the length of the submerged net, she changed course and advanced.

"Get ready," Lisa hollered over the growl of the engines.

Tawd held a new line and hook. He stood poised and beamed at Rodriguez. "I don't even have to gloat. In the clutch, it's always me they want."

"Now Tawd!" Lisa barked.

He twirled his wrist like he had a hundred times before, then released the line, rebar leading the trajectory through the air. It splashed its entry into the dark water with a distinct swoosh. Tawd gave a little tug and started to laugh. It was like he bragged, first try, every time. The weighty green filament breached the surface. Tawd kept the tension while Rodriguez wrapped the lead end of line around the windlass. The captain adjusted for drift, but otherwise kept the ship steady.

"I need floats up here," Lisa called. One of the crew ran the prepared coil of floats to her. "You ready to cut it, Tawd?"

He was already leaned over the side of the ship with the makeshift pruning shears, a natural bead-dreaded arborist at sea. Lisa tied the floats to the net. When they were secure, she nodded at Tawd.

Three quick pulls of the blade on the net and the tension gave way with a resounding crack. It sounded like a .22 going off. The floats were quickly yanked below the surface. One, two, three, the crew counted. Pop, pop, pop, the floats reemerged.

"Someone keep their eyes on these and holler if we drift to close. Everybody else, you know the drill." She waved her hand above her head like a helicopter. The universal signal for 'let's get 'er going.'

A line of four crew members formed along where the net broke the surface and was hitched to the windlass. Each of them wore bright yellow waders, suspenders suspended over their shoulders and clipped to the back of their pants. They looked like a lineup of wedgies waiting to happen. Tawd heaved on the net and each of the others followed suit. After a few pulls they began working in unison as Rodriguez organized the net into weaved rows on the deck.

The weathered skull and cross-bone flag clapped overhead as if it were cheering them on. Lisa clung to its pole and leaned out to sea; eyes glued to the net to report in advance anything that might be coming up.

"We've got movement down there," she spoke into the radio. She glanced at the bridge. "We're going to need another body down here to record."

With each determined pull, the black shadow climbed closer to the surface. Its tail flapped side to side. The thin grey torso shivered in violent outbursts.

Through the gates of the knotted filament, blooded at the gills, a soft rectangular head, a single bulging eye on each side, struggled desperately to regain freedom.

"Get the knives ready," Lisa ordered.

Rodriguez grabbed the knife bucket from beside the equipment locker and ran them over to the bosun.

"We have a hammerhead snagged at the gills," Lisa reported.

Julian appeared on deck, clipboard in hand. "Where do you want me?"

She pointed at the windlass. "You measure, the media people will snap a picture, then back into the water it goes—"

"Now, now, now!" Tawd shouted, not quite angrily, but with definite urgency.

The shark flailed under human prodding. Only a youngling, but already four feet long, it took two crew to pull it over the gunwale and keep it held down on the deck. Somebody splashed it with a bucket of water.

Lisa approved. "Keep it coming."

The bucket was tossed over the side of the Abbey again. When it had filled with seawater the five gallon pail was pulled up by it's rope, hand over hand, to the deck.

Untangled from the net, subdued by Tawd and another crew member, the hammerhead calmed, or at least stopped fighting. Its gills continued to quiver. Each bucket rinsed away the blood, but a steady trickle remained. Its mouth opened and closed in cautious rhythm, each time exposing its razor fangs. Julian laid the measuring tape and recorded the length. The media crew snapped a photo, first of the shark and then another of the male claspers in order to note the sex. One more bucket was splashed on the animal then two of the crew muckled onto it, lifted the shark waist high, and shuffled back toward the stern. They crouched to get as close to the surface of the water as possible then dropped the predator in, head first.

"One down, who knows how many more to go," Lisa said. She waved her arm again. "Let's get this thing up."

Tawd was already on the line, pulling, not gaining anything, but making a spectacle nonetheless. The two crew who released the hammerhead returned to help with the haul.

Most of the animals retrieved were crabs and barnacles and bullseye puffers which could be freed without stopping the momentum of the net coming up. Occasionally, however, an overlooked jellyfish would sting an exposed arm, or a struggling shark would slap the knife from the hand that was trying to cut it free and end up sticking a hand or puncturing a thigh. This most certainly interrupted the flow of things. Still, everybody wanted to be in on the action, if not for the excitement of actually doing something, being up front meant a better chance of being seen in one of the videos. Fifteen minutes of fame from all the two-hundred and seventy-five thousand internet followers closely monitoring the Legion's social media feed.

The crew worked tirelessly for nearly an hour. They'd reached the end of the first half of the net and were preparing to haul the anchor onboard. Rodriguez maintained the steady pull of the windlass to support most of the weight. The few bare patches of the clay-caked anchor glistened under the sun. Tawd shook his head in disgust. He leaned over the side of the ship, secured the anchor in his grip, and yanked it onto the deck. The echoic gong was hallow.

"This is a brand-new anchor," he said, eyes inspecting the clean welds. "I don't even want to know what's caught in the other half."

Lisa picked up the radio and called the bridge. "Can we send the panga team to get started on the other piece while we start processing this net?"

Piles of soaked forest green multi filament lay on top of piles of soaked forest green multi filament. The leaded sinker line used to keep the netting taut to the bottom of the sea was tangled with the yellow float rope used to keep the net stretched toward the surface.

Rodriguez stepped from the windlass and immediately tripped. He groaned.

"Goddammit Rody," Tawd cursed. "You're a liability, you know that."

"Come 'on, Rod," Lisa sighed. "Please, for the love of god, do not walk around this deck with a knife in your hand."

He spoke, staring at the mess around him. "It's not my fault," he whined. "This stuff gets tangled in everything." The thin line wove around the cleats of his boots and between his ankles, and now, because he fell in it, around the buttons of his trousers. He started the slow process of picking away the line and arranging his body so not to become more entangled. Of all things, he was fairly proficient at this task, as his ensnarement occurred almost daily—and not entirely his fault.

Tripping was a risk, if the only one, in working the windlass. It's where all the netting first arrived on deck. From there he was surrounded in layers upon layers of the stuff as he worked back and forth laying the netting down for easier processing.

Boots free, he pushed himself off the ground, and before Tawd could warn him, Rodriguez was face first flat on the deck. The crew burst out laughing. "Those damned buttons," someone joked.

Even Lisa couldn't contain her bashful gasp.

Ed appeared from around the fire equipment locker. "What's so funny?" He set a five-gallon bucket on the deck. The thing looked like it just went mudding, the sides were caked so thick with sludge from the sea. "Chef sent up some new knives to get this net finished."

"Don't let Rody near those," Tawd sneered.

Rodriguez propped himself on his elbows.

"Jesus Christ," Ed said before anyone else noticed the fist-sized pool of blood; before anyone noticed the mess that was Rodriguez's face and hairless chin.

He dabbed his lip. "I think I bit it," he said, examining the red on his fingers.

"Come with me," Ed said. He crouched to help him up.

Rodriguez raised his hand and cried as Ed swatted it away. "Ow!"

"Gross. Not with that hand. The one without the blood. Come on, I'll bring you down to the mess and get you cleaned up." He looked at Lisa. "We're going to send out the panga team to get a head start on the other half. There's no way we can pull it up with the deck in the state that it is."

She bit her lip to hold back a frown, gave Ed the thumbs up, and turned to her deck crew. "You heard the first mate, time to start processing this mess." She hummed. "And better make that fast. I don't like how fresh that anchor was." She lifted a section of the multi filament at her feet, rubbed it between her fingers. "How new this net feels. There's something off here. Something—wrong."

Julian pointed to the float rope lying in the centre of the deck. His gaze illuminated a yellow float scribbled with black Sharpie. "Do these usually come up with graffiti on them?" He asked of no one in particular. He stepped over the netting and picked the float he was talking about. He turned it over in his hands. "Says right here: Go home Legion!"

Lisa snatched it from him and examined the writing. She flicked her wrist, snapped open her Havalon knife, and sliced the float rope. She nodded to the bridge. "Someone up there is going to want this," she said.

As she wandered toward the ladder, Julian heard her mutter "Bad, bad feeling about this." When she cleared earshot, Julian asked, "That was weird, wasn't it?"

"Just grab a knife and give us a hand," Tawd said. He kicked over one of the empty buckets and set it upside down for a seat. He fingered through the five-gallon gaggle of knives and selected a paring knife with a purple handle. He began cutting at the floats. "The paring knives work best, even though all these chumps think the bigger ones do." He waved the little knife in an arch to encapsulate the rest of the crew.

Julian selected a paring knife from the bucket, its white handle faded grey with use. He shoved aside the netting that was piled over the fore cabin hatch and plunked down on the metal cover. "Teach me your ways, master Tawd," he said.

Tawd didn't even snigger.

"For real," Julian said. "Teach me. I want to help." Julian circled his blade like he would have a finger if he was hurrying someone along. "I'm an engineer, remember. If you don't have the time to do it right the first time, where are you going to find the time to do it over again?"

Tawd grabbed the float rope between two unprocessed floats. He rested the knife flush against one of them. Tawd flicked the blade through the thin black filament securing the float in place, then looked up and narrowed his eyes at Julian. "You're not an engineer." He set his blade to the next float and repeated his task. He cut a few more loose. When he started to speak again he didn't bother looking directly at Julian. "I don't know how they find this so difficult. It's common sense. Cut the little filaments, little effort, then slide all the floats off at the end. You even get to reuse the line if you want. The way they hack through everything is three times the effort and ten times the mess. Set. Flick. Done."

Julian mimicked Tawd's effort, and almost immediately, fell into a rhythm like a pair of factory workers on the line. Flick, next, flick, next, flick, next. After they'd amassed a small mountain of float rope and floats, Tawd pulled the black Rubbermaid to his side and set the pile therein. He cut the large line at the last float, held the yellow football, and yanked the float rope free. It was the sound of a hundred tennis balls bouncing far out to sea.

Tawd watched the rest of the crew in disgust. "We'll process ninety percent of this net before they finish those three metres it's taking four of them to get through."

Two of the crew, whom Tawd was referring, stuck out their tongue. One of them raised his middle finger. Julian lowered his eyes.

"Why are you always picking on everyone? We're all out here doing the same thing, aren't we?"

This time he got a response.

Tawd yanked at another section of net. "I'm not picking on anyone. They're just soft, is all. Eco-tourists out here to notch their resumes. Rich kids on daddy's dime, dying to get back to shore to update their Instagram with all the hero shots of the work they've been doing out here." He sliced the blade through each filament as he spoke. Each word was accented with a flick of the wrist and another float freed. "See, if they even gave two cares about the animals that were caught in this net, they'd realize that the faster we get this section sorted out, the faster we'd be onto the piece that's still out there—and who knows what's dying in the interim. Every minute we're playing Adidas's toady on deck, we're not saving lives."

Julian collected the line that Tawd was cutting and sliced it where Tawd had stopped. He placed the pile in the Rubbermaid and pulled the line like he'd been shown. Plop-plop-plop, tennis balls all over again. "What do you mean, 'playing Adidas's toady'?"

"Are you serious?"

Julian shrugged. "We're like mushrooms down there in the engine room: Kept in the dark and fed crap."

This earned a grin from Tawd.

"I have no idea what goes on up here," Julian pleaded.

Tawd nodded. He pointed his knife toward the stern. "You know all those Parley bags piled up back there?" He didn't wait for Julian to acknowledge, only continued slicing at the float rope. "Parley is owned by Adidas. We're just a bunch of lemmings they use to increase their profit margins."

"Parley? Lemmings? Speak English, dude. What does our campaign have anything to do with it?"

Tawd set the purple paring knife beside his bucket seat. He rested his hands on his knees, took a deep breath, and let it expire.

Before he could speak, Julian added, "And don't be a dick about it. I'm just trying learn."

Tawd scoffed. "We find the gill nets, right? We drag the waters burning all this fuel in a decommissioned boat we've rehabbed, so who knows what kind of environmental damage we're leaving in our wake. Then when the ray snaps and the floats pop up, we circle around another half dozen times, usually getting snagged up on ourselves, and the damage that causes to whatever remains of the seal around the prop and leak whatever else—"

Julian stared blankly. His engines didn't leak. At least they didn't leak that he was aware of.

"Okay," Tawd said. He realized Julian wasn't keeping up and began again. "We find the gill nets, pull them up, right? Then we strip them of the lead and the floats, like we're doing now." He waved his hand over the mess dramatically. He really seemed to relish this emperor disdain. "Once the Parley bags are filled with the clean multi filament, we ship them to whatever third-world country Adidas has just acquired a new factory in—"

The other crew on deck had slowed their processing and were listening. Tawd realized this and shifted his posture to capitalize on the attention.

"They melt down the nets, the plastics, or whatever they do to make the material viable for spinning into shoes and shorts and hats and whatever. They call it their Parley line: Sustainable feel-good running shoes for only two-hundred bucks a pair—straight back into their corporate coffers."

"That's disgusting," one of the eavesdroppers stated plainly.

"What's disgusting?" It was Lisa. Nobody saw her return to the deck.

"That we're doing all this work—all this volunteer work—for Adidas," Tawd snarled.

She glowered at him. He picked up the net and continued processing. Julian did the same.

"We don't do this for Adidas," she said. "We do this for the oceans. We do it for the lives of all the animals who live in them. That's who we do it for."

"And what for Adidas' profit, then?"

"We're recycling the garbage we pull. Would you rather we throw it away in San Felipe? The locals would be all over it in a second—and even sooner have the nets repaired and back in the water."

Someone said, "But Adidas is Evil-corp."

Lisa sat down and picked up her own section of net. "Maybe they're trying to turn their image around. People can do that, can't they?"

"Not corporations," said someone else. "All they care about it money."

For a while, nobody spoke. All the crew worked silently, slicing at the filament, and stripping the lines of the floats. The earlier rivalry between Tawd and the rest had settled into contemplative reflection. They worked like this until Rodriguez and Ed returned to the deck.

"Wow," Ed said. He smiled at the buzz of his little worker bees. "I've never seen you all so focused at getting these nets finished. Good job guys and gals."

He caught eyes with Julian, who bashfully shook his head. Ed pitched his eyebrows, then shrugged. "Well, now that it's safe for Rody to be back on deck, what do you say we bag up all this netting and move on to the other half?" He raised his chin at Rodriguez. "Grab some of those fresh Parley bags from the locker and bring them up here, will ya?"

Rodriguez disappeared around the corner. Lisa changed the subject.

"Any word on the panga team?"

Ed nodded as his face drained of all joviality. "It's not good. They pulled up three totoaba in the first ten feet."

Tawd slapped his bucket across the deck. "I knew it," he said sharply.

Everybody looked to where the panga was drifting alongside the section of submerged netting. The two men in the panga stood, knees bent, hunched at the waist. It was a delicate act to haul the net onboard. As they balanced, they worked their gloved hands to surgically cut free the tangled monster-sized fish. The three carcasses they'd already pulled up, lay stacked on top of each other in the hull of their little boat and took up the majority of the standing space. Their caudal fins hung over the gunwale. Sweat poured from the brows of each exhausted labourer.

As the crew on board the Abbey watched, the two men on the panga cut the next totoaba free. It took both of them to lift the fish from the water and add it to the pile. The carcass slapped the others and shook the panga. The pair threw their arms out for balance, little wings tipping up and down until they regained their equilibrium.

Ben yelled up to the bosun. "We're not going to be able to pull them all in." He looked at the four fish in his boat, then down into the black abyss. "They have to be at least a hundred pounds each." He knelt down and ran his hand along the fish they'd just pulled in. "Uncut, too."

Lisa picked up her radio and replied through the airwaves. "What do you mean, 'uncut'?"

"Uncut, like they still have their swim bladders. This is a fresh catch."

She let the radio fall to her waist. Ben continued.

"Means they'll have eyes on us if they're not already on their way here."

Half a dozen hands rose to their respective eyebrows as the crew on-board the Abbey scanned the waters all around the ship.

"I'll have the captain right the ship and we'll get the net hooked up to the windlass. You guys will have to get up here and give us a hand."

"Roger that," Ben replied. He looked at the totoaba, again. "What do you want us to do with these?"

Lisa thought a moment, humming as she did. "Once we get the ship turned around, pass them up by the stern. Captain has different protocols for the totoaba. She'll tell us what she wants us to do." She turned from the panga and looked to the bridge. Then as an afterthought, she clapped a couple times to get Ben's attention. She yelled, "Stay off the radio for now."

A rested hand on Julian's shoulder startled him.

"This might be the time you disappear to the engine room," Tawd said.

Some of the other crew chuckled.

"It's going to get messy up here and Tamara will lose her mind if you get that smell on your clothes and track it down there."

"That's one thing she's not hippie about," someone added.

Julian laughed. He picked up an armful of multi filament and shoved it into a Parley bag. "Well, thanks for letting play deck crew for a little bit."

Chapter Ten: Infatuation

Below deck, down in the engine room, Tamara crouched knees deep in the bilge. A hose sprouted from the floor and pulsed with rhythmic digestion. It ran above the yellow fuel lines—which were secured to the bulk-head—then down to a pump where a second section of hose returned to the hull.

Her arms were covered in sludge. A single smear divided her face, the result of an earlier arm brush. Julian hesitated at the door as if he was considering retreating to the tool room and remaining there until Tamara had finished whatever she was doing, but before he could escape, Tamara spotted him and beamed. Julian's face twisted as he tried to make sense of it. She was covered in sludge, yet still smiling. Glowing even. And beautiful.

She wiped her face with the backside of her hand, then pointed to the small pump reverberating in the corner. "I got it working," she yelled above the churning engines. "It's a blast!"

The little gas-powered Honda roared with excitement, sucking sludge from the bilge, massaging it up its hose, over the fuel line, and back into the belly of the ship.

The muddled expression possessing Julian's face had Tamara in stitches. He looked like he'd just walked in on a fat kid spooning a tub of margarine into his pie hole: disgusted and intrigued and embarrassed all at the same time, where maybe if he silently retreated one step after the other out of frame, both would be spared the awkward conversation that would ensue.

Tamara laughed. "What am I supposed to do, pump the oil over-board?"

Julian wagged his head in disbelief.

"If you don't want to get dirty, don't. I'm for grease and sludge over fish guts any day!" The mire consuming her ankles and slopped on her clothes was a badge of honour—and she looked satisfied at the fact. "But if you're going to be down here with me, you might as well make yourself useful and shut that thing off."

Julian knelt at the pump and flicked the two-way switch to kill the flow of fuel through the engine. The hoses quit throbbing. The room quieted, if ever so slightly, until an alarm on the other side of the engine room blared. It sounded like an ambulance winding up its wail. The alarm was the same as the one screaming about the generator fire, the one Julian first heard when he boarded the M/V Edward Abbey those few weeks ago. The night of the drowned man. That same alarm from the word 'go.'

Tamara glanced at the control panel. The low engine oil light flashed like vitals monitor during a heart attack.

"Ugh," she said with gall. "Silence that for me, will ya?"

"Shouldn't we investigate?"

She shook her head. "The captain just bumped the ship into reverse is all. That port engine is finicky."

"Just clear it?"

Her brow winced in puzzlement. Tamara was not one to curate her expressions. Nor was she one to clip her words. "What's gotten into you? What's with your timidity all of a sudden? Just press the button. I'd ask you to give me a hand out of here and I'd do it myself, but I know how you feel about getting dirty. Squeamish little boy…kinda cute, like the port side generator." She winked and let her mouth gape playfully. She set her hands on the floor grates and bounced from the bilge to seated on the ledge. "Come 'on," she said. "I'll supervise to make sure you don't accidentally blow up the ship or sink us or something."

It wasn't that Julian was worried, he was preoccupied. Swimming. All that chatter about Adidas profiting from their conservation efforts; if even their campaign wasn't some calculated ruse, a magician's misdirection, keeping the public's attention away from another corporate exploit. That and the alarm triggering the suppressed memory of the drowned boy. For what?

Julian rested his finger on the flashing oil level light and another on the clear button. Tamara watched him with increasing concern. He pressed them simultaneously and the alarm quit whining. The engine room was again only the rumble of the generator, the whirl of the exhaust fan, and the steady growl of the port side V12.

Tamara looped the pump hose around a hook in the corner. With each coil, globs of bilge splattered on the bulkhead wall. Every time she wrapped it around, bilge splattered on her already covered coveralls. In three successive clangs, Julian had replaced the floor grates. When Tamara detached the second hose the pump burped.

"Did you hear that?" she yelled above the engine room's accustomed decibel. "The little guy just thanked me for feeding him."

"Don't forget to rinse him out like the last crew did."

"Are you kidding me? Oil is the best treat for this little engine that could. If I dropped it in the ocean and put it back on the shelf with nothing, it still wouldn't corrode for the amount of grease I put through him."

Julian wagged his head. "You're weird."

She winked. "Sexy weird."

Tamara spread her greasy arms and threatened to hug him.

It was a reflex, but when she lurched, his arms sprang from his side, palms open, fingers stretched wide like a crossing guard stopping traffic—only his innocent defence, his open palms, behaved like heat seeking missiles and landed directly on Tamara's chest. Not even flat-like; his hands were cupped. Like a junior feeling up a girl for the first time and resting his hands over the bra.

Tamara's reaction was ferocious. Her arms snapped across her chest as her body recoiled from Julian's frozen touch.

"I—I—I—" he stuttered.

"Never in my life!" Tamara screamed.

"I'm so, so sorry, Tamara."

She held her chest as if she were clutching a baby. "Do you know how much harassment I have to deal with working around all these guys to begin with?" Her eyes narrowed with her flushing face. She stepped toward Julian, slowly, vengefully.

Julian shuffled his retreat, arms raised.

She pointed toward the engine room door, "That's out there in the real world." She stabbed her thumb into the skull and crossbones emblem on her coveralls. "Not Trident Legion!" A crazed look possessed her.

Julian swallowed hard. He shook nervously. He didn't speak.

"We're supposed to be a breed above the rest. Evolved. Respectful. Harbingers of hope, dammit!"

The wall behind Julian closed upon him. His hands felt for it. Backed into the corner and nowhere to go; literally.

"And from you of all people, Julian. You're the only person on this ship who hasn't made an unwanted advance." She stood a foot in front of him.

"Tamara, I'm so—so sorry."

She glared. "Yeah, you said that already."

He remained postered against the wall; shoulders pressed into the yellow fuel lines behind him. He tried to speak, "I—," but before he could apologize a third time, Tamara pecked his cheek with her lips. No sooner had she kissed him did she twirl around and march toward the engine room door.

First mortified, now stunned, Julian remained where he'd become part of the ship's structure. His eyes were silver dollars.

Tamara laughed. "You guys are so pathetic." She pointed straight at him. "As if I'm going to complain about the most action I've gotten in months. I should be thanking you."

Julian relaxed a little. Whether he meant it or not, the next words out of Julian's mouth were, "I mean—I could do it again."

It happened so fast, everything going black. Julian didn't realize it at first, but he wore Tamara's bilge rag on his face. He shook it off and caught it. It's when he started gagging. The smell of moulding kitty litter clung to his skin. His mouth tasted like the swamp from behind his house when he was a kid. He convulsed so convincingly for a moment; a flutter of concern singed Tamara. Julian threw the rag on the floor grates and braced himself for the purge.

Tamara howled. She nearly fell to the ground herself. "You are so-ooo, so dramatic."

His breaths laboured. He was certainly going to spew. It was right there...then, by chance, he exhaled long enough to compose himself. Julian wiped his mouth with his sleeve. He used the other arm to run across his eyes. He squinted at Tamara. "You're a witch."

Tamara spun the wheel on the engine room hatch and released the mandibles. She popped her lips. "I've been called worse."

Again, Julian couldn't help but smile.

"Are you just going to cower there in the corner or are you going to get in here and clean yourself up?" She jerked her face in disgust. "Yuck. You're filthy."

He gave her the once over. Grease clung to Tamara's hair. Her face crusted with sludge. From waist down was clumped and soaked and clinging to her legs. He shivered. "I'm filthy? Okay, Tamara."

They laughed in the way the spark of first loves laugh when they're certain something has happened, but unsure in the same vein, afraid to draw attention to it in case it might disappear forever.

"I'm going to change into something else," Tamara said. "Want to meet in the mess in ten and you can tell me everything that's going on up there?"

Julian collapsed in the swivel chair behind his desk in his engineer cabin. His feet danced along the carpet until he was spinning. He looked like a guy who just received a kiss from a colleague he never thought about relationally before, but in a matter of minutes convinced himself that it all made perfect sense. He inhaled as if he was breathing strawberry Herbal Essence from her hair. He pressed his foot against the filing cabinet and let go a solid push. As impulsive as this final twirl had been, he quickly slammed on the brakes. If Ed or Tamara were to walk in on him, he'd have some serious explaining to do—that, and the ridiculous grin on his face.

Trying to compose himself, Julian stared at the computer screen. The open document was the handover report Gilles had left him. The same handover report he'd started to read a dozen times, but kept getting interrupted that he never actually finished it. A line on the report jumped out at him: The saltwater inlet elbow has been repaired with epoxy but continues to leak and requires replacement. Julian stroked his chin as if he had a beard. He'd have to look into that soon. All that sludge Tamara siphoned up and around, for sure had to mean a worsening leak.

He looked over his small private quarters with approval: a sink in the corner; the desk where he sat; the filing cabinet; the locker; the bunk beds where he slept topside, even though Gilles wouldn't be back for another six months or so and if he wanted the bottom bunk he could have commandeered it no problem. He liked the top bunk better anyway. Not too bad for not being an engineer, playing Chief Engineer.

"Admiring your kingdom, Chief?"

The girl's voice nearly tipped Julian from the chair where he leaned in dangerous repose. Tamara bit her lip.

"Well, aren't you going to invite me in?"

Julian bumbled his composure and offered his chair for her to sit in; he'd take the seat on the empty bed.

"Still all worried, I see," she mocked. "I mean if you feel really bad about groping me, I guess you could do my laundry. None of this, 'Oh, please take my chair,' fake chivalry. It's got to be something good."

She brushed past him and flung herself on the bottom bunk. Her shirt lifted exposing her midriff.

"These digs are way better than the aft-cabin."

Julian stared at the pale lighted skin beneath her shirt.

Tamara looked up. A soft smile came over her face when she caught him staring. She settled her head on the pillow and adjusted her shirt. "So, tell me what's going on up there—or, maybe something more interesting, why you've been so spacey this last little bit. What's up?"

Julian rubbed his palms over his face, trying to squeeze the romantic ideas from his mind. "I don't know," he said finally.

"Sure you don't."

"It's not just one thing, but now what I just found out, and I'm sure it's all related—"

"It's, it's, it's. Spit it out already."

"Did you know we're pulling up these nets for an Adidas initiative?"

Tamara propped herself up on her elbows. "Ohhh."

"But, that's not all. I mean, how many Vaquita are left? 20? 14? When was the last time you saw one? I've never seen one—and these are the dolphins we hope to rescue from the endangered species list? How long will that take? If it's even possible. How many years are we going to keep coming back, burning all this fuel from our leaky little ship? It's not like the locals are even trying to catch the Vaquita, they're after that other fish, the toto—"

"Totoaba."

"Totoaba, right. And we steal those from the fishermen. These people are just trying to feed their families. It's not like they're some corporate fishing outfit—that's us, we're the corporate bumpkins pimping ourselves to a conglomerate, and doing all this fundraising for what? To keep our own bureaucracy alive? Can we even save the Vaquita? And should we? Aren't most of the species that have ever existed extinct? And them long before we ever showed up. This isn't the Faroes. It's not like the locals are barbarically slaughtering in celebration. They're fishing." He gave an agitated push and spun in his chair. "I don't know," he continued after he came to a stop. "It just seems like it's a lot of moving parts, a lot of money, a lot of wasted resources, for what?"

A resonant thud pounded above. Both Tamara and Julian smarted their bodies. Tamara swung her feet over the side of the bed and sat up.

"What the heck was that?" she said.

Julian wondered the same thing.

Chapter Eleven: Totoaba

Topside the crew bustled to prepare the deck for what the panga team anticipated would be the mother load of all hauls. Four uncut, one-hundred-pound totoabas, had been retrieved from the first ten feet of the gill net. Nothing good could come of that. Up until this point on the Milagro campaign, all the totoaba they'd brought up had already been harvested for their swim bladders and left tangled to rot where they'd been caught. It was messy work, but the crew didn't mind. Each haul meant one less net in the water. No more animals would be sacrificed for the greed of some filthy fishermen. Nevertheless, a fresh catch had everybody on edge.

The next totoaba was passed from the panga and four crew members struggled to carry it to where the other had slipped from their grip and smacked the deck.

Rodriguez grunted as they quick shuffled in unison.

Someone else strained to find hope in the situation and offered, "Maybe there won't be any more—the first half of the net didn't have any."

While the transfer of the totoaba carcass's continued, Rodriguez and Tawd got the net hooked up to the windlass. Rodriguez assumed his position and pressed the foot pedal to start the motor turning. "Can't imagine what it would have been like pulling up these nets before we had the windlass installed," he said.

Nobody replied. All eyes were trained on the ominous shadows rising from the water.

"I need two guys beside me," Lisa commanded, pointing to the eyelet in the gunwale where the net was run through. "You're going to cut them free as they're pulled up, and pass them to the panga team. Ben, you guys will run them back as far as you can and line them up beside the others. Not one of these goes back in the water, captain's orders."

The teams moved into their assigned positions.

"First one's up," she hollered. She sounded like a line-cook at a restaurant.

Rodriguez released his foot from the pedal. The windlass stopped turning. The team on the gunwale cut the fish free and passed it to the panga team. They shuffled the carcass back beside the other four already lined up on the deck.

Ben whimpered. "That's five."

Lisa spun her finger. This cued Rodriguez on the pedal. The windlass fired up and the teams were at it again. For the next two hours it was windlass on, stop, cut the totoaba free, pass it over, line it up, and windlass on...repeat.

It was high afternoon and the crew had pulled in thirty-four freshly caught totoaba—fully intact. No one knew how many were still waiting to be hauled up. Nobody knew how long the net actually was. The longest one they'd retrieved to date was some record breaking four-hundred and seventy metres.

The heat from above soured the dead fish and cursed the air vile. Everybody except Rodriguez had rotated through the positions of puller, cutter, and runner. Everybody except Rodriguez were covered in sweat and sea water—which are pretty much the same beneath the scorching sun—and dripped with the slimy totoaba film. Only a single report had been run up to the bridge since the start of this mega-pull. Not even Lisa used the radio. Julian asked why it was so important to keep the airwaves silent.

"It's Mexico," Ed said, as if Julian should have known what 'It's Mexico,' implied.

He, Tamara, the captain, and Ed were observing the action from above. Tamara's disbelief was too much for her hard-fast rule to never to be topside when a catch was coming in.

Ed continued. "We work with the government."

Julian shrugged.

"Like officially they're our partners on the campaign. It's the only way they'd let us put our ships in their waters. But more probably is they have a cut of the trade and want to make sure we're not interfering too much."

"Only we've never come across a fresh catch like this," the captain added.

"Don't we usually report to PROFEPA when we come across one of the totoaba?" Julian asked. It was an innocent question.

"Yeah," Ed said. "But not like this. All the totoaba we've recovered have always been gutted by the time we've found them. There's like three-hundred grand lying on the deck right now if we turn them in the way that they are." He sucked his cheeks. "See what I'm getting at? How would it look if the highly-esteemed Trident Legion Conservation Organization retrieved an abandoned gill net from the sea, all the poached fish fully intact, and we turned them over to the same community who actively deployed these nets in the first place with the sole intention of catching totoaba just so they can sell the swim bladders to China?"

The captain picked up the radio and told Lisa to come to the bridge. This was the first time since the crew had begun this section of net that the radio was used. Lisa hustled up the ladder and popped her head inside the hatchway.

"Captain," she said reporting dutifully.

"We need the swim bladders out before we call this in."

White draped Lisa's face. "Captain?" she asked.

"I know some of the crew won't be up for the task, but it needs to be done. You and Tawd do it while the others continue pulling in the net. Slit the belly and cut out the bladders. Make sure you pierce them a few times so they don't float. Then toss them overboard." Her words were stone.

Lisa swallowed but didn't speak. Her eyes struggled to digest the order. Tamara excused herself and disappeared into the ship.

"We can't hand them over the way they are," the captain said. "You know that. We'll just be feeding the machine we're trying to stop."

Lisa nodded.

"I need this done like ten minutes ago."

The captain returned her attention to the happenings of the deck. Lisa descended the ladder. The two men, Ed and Julian, flashed a glance at each other with arched eyebrows.

Down below, Lisa pulled Tawd aside and told him their task. He looked up to the captain, nodded, then picked up a knife. The rest of the crew, faces puzzled and disgusted and reluctant all at the same time, were arranged to keep the assembly line moving.

A tiny splash beside the ship, something like a clutch purse dropped in a pool, provoked a ripple of shivers among the crew. Tawd had four bellies opened, but only this last one did he remove the swim bladder, stab it, and toss it over the side.

"How do you want to do this?" he asked. "I can go along and get them all slit, you follow behind and pierce the bladders, then throw them overboard? Or the other way around?"

She didn't answer, only flipped open her own knife, and started sawing at a swim bladder.

"The ends justify the means, Lisa. Time to Trident Legion the heck up."

She pierced the organ several times then threw it over the side.

The windlass spun with hums and pauses that sounded like an emergency S-O-S. The crew on the gunwale retrieved the fish, passed them to the running crew who lined them up in front of Tawd and Lisa, who in turn, executed their specific role in the sequence to remove and sink the golden organs. California gulls circled the Abbey in predatory ambition. Their mew calls, long and drawn, netted the ship.

"Well," Lisa said, eyes shielded to observe the birds overhead. "If they didn't know we had their net up already, they certainly know now."

Tawd continued the robotic movements with his blade. He hummed as he worked and one could easily imagine how he might have been instructing his morbid task: Grip the tail, lift, knife the piss hole, slit; again. His cold efficiency bothered Lisa.

"You're too comfortable with the blade to have not done this before."

He continued humming. It sounded near the cries of the gulls. Head down focused on the slitting of fish bellies, and in a causal tone, Tawd spoke. "Is anybody going to call in those boats approaching?"

"Boats?" Lisa surveyed the horizon.

Tawd pointed his knife toward the bow, six o'clock, starboard side.

Absorbed in the task, none of the crew, except Tawd, had noticed the boats skipping across the water some two-hundred metres out.

"Shoot," Lisa muttered. "Do you think they're poachers?"

Tawd moved to the next row of totoaba carcasses.

"I think we better hurry up and harvest these, is what I think."

Lisa grabbed at her radio and called the bridge. She waved her hands overhead then pointed toward the two boats. The distance made it difficult to determine whether they were PROFEPA boats bouncing along, or enraged poachers aggressively mogulling their advance.

"Bosun, this is Bridge," the captain said.

Lisa looked up.

"The starboard vessels are friendlies."

"Whatever that means," Tawd sneered.

Lisa hushed him. "What do you want us to do, Captain?"

The captain picked up the broadband and waved it at Lisa, who fumbled at her side to grip the lanyard then pulled her own broadband from her pocket.

"These don't transmit on their frequencies," the captain said.

Tawd continued with his task. He clicked his tongue at Lisa and bobbed his chin over his shoulder. The rest of the crew stood stunned at the unfolding drama.

"Get to work!" she barked.

Lisa had never yelled at the crew before. Rodriguez stumbled back. Everybody smarted their attention.

"Those boats are already here," she warned. "We need as many 'oabas up as we can get. Out of the water, chop chop."

The giggle behind Lisa belonged to Tawd. She glared at him, then back to the crew who remained idle.

She clapped her hands. "Let's go! Let's go! Let's go!"

Rodriguez huffed but resumed the pedal. The boats had closed a hundred metres and would be on the Abbey in minutes. Tawd realized the same thing and quit slitting to start puncturing the bladders. The two of them worked furiously to sink the bladders before the PROFEPA boats arrived. They tossed the bladders opposite where the boats approached from, port side, hoping they'd tie up from the way they came.

"We have a live one!" Ben said.

"Throw it back."

The shrill whine of the RIB's engines echoed over the deck, still, the live totoaba splashing its return to the water softened the tension in the air. At least one was saved.

The boats reached the Abbey as two more totoaba were added to the row of dead fish. Ed slowly descended from the bridge to the deck. He snapped his fingers at Rodriguez to join him. He needed a translator.

Competing words spoken in escalating tones made it impossible for Rodriguez to know who was in charge and what to relay to Ed. These uniformed men seemed to be in an argument and were quite excited about it.

"Oi!" Rodriguez chirped. He raised his arms. What followed was a rapid fire of Spanish sentences which Ed couldn't keep up with.

The PROFEPA crew silenced themselves, however, a signal, a nonchalant checking of the chin from the one who was likely in charge to the driver of their sister boat, had it motor around to the other side of the Abbey. The efforts of the Trident Legion crew were immediately halted. Lisa and Tawd quickly sheathed their knives and replaced in their hands, a clipboard and a measuring tape. They began sizing up the carcasses they'd only moments before been cutting up. The charade included stepping over each fish, laying the tape measure, and writing down the length in centimetres. Tawd stole a glance over the gunwale. All the bladders they'd thrown overboard had sunk. At least there was that they didn't have to worry about.

"They want to know why we didn't call in the net," Rodriguez said.

Ed's brow furrowed. He raised his hands in surrender offering. He looked at the officials and said, "We just found it." He pointed to Lisa and her clipboard, to Tawd and his measuring tape, and to the rest of the crew stationary in their positions. "We were writing the report so we could provide an accurate count."

The uniformed men looked at Rodriguez and waited.

Four pairs of eyes narrowed at the explanation. They stared at Ed. The man who instructed the other boat to investigate to the Abbey's port, presumably the first mate, bugged his eyes. He raised his voice so loud that spittle flew from his mouth as he fired back at Rodriguez.

"Maybe we should ask how they just happened upon us," Tawd said.

Lisa spoke in throated tone, teeth clenched. "Don't make it worse, Tawd."

The man quit yelling, and Rodriguez, calm, yet almost annoyed, told Ed that the captain should have called them as soon as the first totoaba was pulled out of the water.

"That's it," Ed asked. "All that yelling, all that animation?"

Rodriguez shrugged. "We're a passionate people."

Ed nodded. He clasped his hands together in front of him and bowed slightly. "We meant no disrespect," he said. "It won't happen again. You can come aboard and assess for your selves." And Rodriguez translated.

Lisa couldn't help herself. "Ed."

He shook his head as dismissively as she had over Tawd's remark. The swell of the sea pushed the RIB onto the Abbey, then rolled off. Ed showed them were to tie on and lowered the accommodation ladder. The first mate threw the painter line to Rodriguez, who dropped it, which then had to be retrieved, and thrown again. When he caught the painter line's carabiner, he attached it to the stanchion above the ladder. Ed greeted each of them as they boarded the Abbey. The captain glowered from above.

"Ed!" Lisa yelled again. This time with urgency. Anybody who wasn't on the bow immediately turned their concern to her. He shuffled past the PROFEPA crew toward her cry.

She shook her arm frantically in the direction of the net slung over the gunwale. "They're taking the fish, Ed, they're taking the fish."

Sure enough, the second PROFEPA boat had sidled up to the net. The four-man crew worked with joyous energy as they leaned over their inflated gunwales cutting free a totoaba and letting it slip into the hull of their own boat. Splashes erupted as a live fish broke the surface. The men tried after it, too, to get it into their boat.

"That's a live one, Ed," Lisa said, pointing desperately.

"Let out some slack," he commanded.

She must have had the idea at the same time, because before he finished his instruction, Lisa was on the windlass and unwinding the net.

Curses rolled over the side of the ship. "Chingada-Madre!" One of them said, raising and shaking his fist in the air.

"Enough!" Ed barked at the men. "Enough." They scowled but quit protesting. He turned to Lisa, rested his hands on her shoulders and looked straight into her eyes. Her face softened so much she looked like she would cry. "We did what we could," he said calmly. "That's what we're here to do."

A sob escaped her mouth. "I was just murdering fish."

"They were already dead, Lisa. You were stealing money from the poachers is what you were doing."

Her arm shot up and shook violently at the net. "That one wasn't dead!" She choked.

Ed threw his arms around her and pulled her close into his chest.

"That one wasn't," she said, and began to cry.

Ed squeezed. The deck was silent but for the gull's overhead and the idling PROFEPA boats. Even Tawd looked away. Eventually, the solemn moment was interrupted by the laughter of the PROFEPA team below. Lisa's body tensed under Ed's embrace.

The gulls yelped.

"I need to go inside," she whispered.

Ed was already leading her from the deck. When they were out of earshot, Tawd picked up the broadband and called the captain.

"What do you want us to do?" he asked.

The radio cracked, then sighed. All eyes were on the bridge.

"You did good," the captain said. "PROFEPA will take it from here."

"Should we pass them what we have?"

The captain gave the affirmative and Tawd turned to face the crew.

"Alright," he said, chest puffed up just a little. "We might not trust them, we might not like it, but as Ed said, we did what we're here to do," he paused. Another carcass slapped the inside of the PROFEPA boat. "And like the Captain affirmed, we did good. You all did good." He looked at Rodriguez. "Except for you Rody, you didn't do anything." Rodriguez glared. Tawd smiled. "I'm just kidding around. We all came together on this one. We've been out here for hours, maybe we should just look at it like they're doing us a favour by pulling in the rest of the net."

"I hope they tip their boat," Ben said.

Tawd laughed. "Here's hoping."

Like a Baptist congregation, everybody amen-ed their agreement.

"Now let's cut ourselves free of the net and start passing these heavy monsters down to the chirpy little Mexicans."

The clash of metal on metal rang out when Rodriguez kicked the covers off the windlass pedals. "You know I'm Mexican, right?"

"Of course, I know. You're chirpiest of them all!"

Everybody chuckled. Tawd clapped his hand on Rodriguez's shoulder and pulled him in. "Come 'on, I'll work up front with you."

For the next hour, the team worked their assembly line in reverse. Instead of pulling net, retrieving the totoaba, and passing them along, the Legion crew lugged the heavy carcasses of dead and mutilated fish, from the Abbey, back to the sea. Well, to the PROFEPA crew, who greedily piled the fish in their own boat. By the end of the day, the count had risen to sixty-four—some forty of whom were retrieved by the Trident Legion and gutted before PROFEPA took over. A handful of totoaba were pulled live, and under the watchful eye of the Abbey's captain, were reluctantly returned to the sea.

Chapter Twelve: Rally

The PROFEPA report stated: It is suspected that the Trident Legion crew recovered the totoaba intact, removed the swim bladders illegally, and have them stored in the hull of their ship, until they can smuggle them out of Mexico.

The irony, of course, is that the Abbey crew held the same suspicions about the PROFEPA outfit. The captain prepared to address the ship. Ed and Lisa fitted themselves with mics, black receiver boxes clipped to their waists, thumb size microphones clipped to their collars. Each of the other crew were sent to their cabins to put on clean Trident Legion t-shirts. When the cameras were rolling everybody needed to look their Sunday best.

Whenever the captain addressed the crew during a morning brief, it was more than a moral-boost. It was fundraising. A pep rally. Propaganda for the people back home, the people with deep pockets who received all the Trident Legion clips via the Five-Bullet-Friday ChumpMail subscription which reminded them that their previous donation has saved X amount of sea life to date, and that their next donation would go directly to saving the Vaquita marina dolphin in the Sea of Cortez, where every day the crew onboard the M/V Edward Abbey risked their lives to defend the oceanic waters from the cartel and poachers alike.

One by one the crew returned, freshly groomed and smiles painted on convincingly. Smiling made a bigger impact on the screen. It appealed on an emotional level: even in the face of danger the Trident Legion volunteer crew remained positive they would succeed.

"Let's get these books and video games stashed before the camera's go live, alright?" Ed said.

A few people wrapped the controller cords around their respective controllers, then the power cord around the Xbox, and tucked them beneath the benches they sat on.

Julian hated the theatrics. It was becoming apparent that even as far back as his minute in the Faroes, everything the Trident Legion did seemed only to fund-raise more money and keep the organization's pockets lined. The volunteers were passionate idealists, but the higher ranking bureaucrats treated the entire campaign like a balance sheet that needed to remain flush regardless whether their actions actually made a positive environmental impact. Julian sat as far outside of the camera angle as possible. Across the mess, Tamara sat opposite, near the tool room door. As soon as the brief was over, Tamara would disappear into the engine room and Julian to his cabin to review the tasks for the day.

"Two minutes," one of the media people warned.

A hush settled over the mess. The collective focus aligned on the stairway where the captain would descend from.

Ed stood centre stage in front of the 50" flat screen TV, microwave, shelf of mugs, and the party-pack bags of Spicy Sweet Chili Doritos—the only variety of Doritos that didn't have animal byproducts in them and thus were vegan approved.

"Look at all your pretty faces," he said. His smile stretched creepily from one ear to the next. Ed knew how to play the game. He scanned the room, and as he did, he sniffed the air. "And boy am I glad you all showered!"

This earned laughter from the audience.

"I just want to thank you, each of you, for your top-notch effort yesterday. It was tough work, and you all did it without complaining."

"And we'd do it again, mate!" Tawd asserted from his seat in the middle of the room.

The rest of the crew clapped along. A few people yelped and wooed and some started banging their open palms on whatever surface was nearby: the table, the wall, the bench. The cameras rolled.

"Now this is what I like to see!" the captain shouted.

The cheering continued as the captain assumed centre stage and made a point of acknowledging each of the crew with a personal glance and re-hearsed appreciative smile.

When the room settled, the captain continued. "We have a great team this campaign." She nodded her head as she spoke. "I'm not supposed to say this, but you guys are the best crew I've ever captained."

The media team panned their cameras over all the flattered faces.

"It really is my honour to work with each and every one of you—" Her eyes settled on a camera and addressed the would-be video patron. "We're a family. And as a family, occasionally, we have to endure some hardships; tough times we wish we didn't have to go through; days like yesterday." She pouted her lips and sighed. "But it's days like yesterday that make us stronger as a family." She slapped the metal counter. "We pulled up eight-hundred metres of net!"

Tawd clapped on the table. The captain pointed at him.

"Exactly! We should be proud of that. We robbed hundreds of thou-sands of dollars right out of the pockets of those poachers, those ruthless evil murderers. And we did it right under their watchful eyes—" She paused. "And we'll do it again."

The mess erupted in monkey wails: Ooo-oo-oo-oo-oo-oo!

"We're not scared, are we?" she asked.

"Heck no!" The collective voice shouted their refrain.

"We're Trident Legion!"

"Yeah we are!"

"Let me put this to you then," she said. "You all worked your butts off yesterday, you deserve a break. You've more than earned it." She nodded her own agreement with the sentiment. "We have two options. We're only a few hours from the harbour—we can head in, give you all a leave pass for town, today could be some R&R."

The red light illuminated on camera number two which was pointed at Tawd. He acted like he was mulling over the option.

"Or, while everybody was catching up on some much needed sleep last night, our radar picked up two very promising targets, positions con-firmed by the navy, directly inside the Vaquita refuge." The captain's eyes glowed above her sinister grin. She looked hungry. Ravenous even. Hard to tell if she was just putting it on for the cameras or if she sincerely loathed the fishermen. She was good. "We can fire up the engines, rip across the open water, and take another crack at those villains." She cupped her clenched fist like a pitcher waiting for the catcher's sign to hurl a knuckle ball.

The mugs on the shelf behind the captain clamoured together, the hands rapping on the tables shook the room so violently.

Tawd was first to affirm, "Let's crush these villains!"

The crew was possessed by predatory eyes.

"My team is ready, captain!" Lisa said, a stink eye fired toward Tawd who returned the nearly imperceptible affront with a kiss of his lips. The cameras didn't catch it, but if they had, this interpersonal drama could easily be edited from the final product.

"You're all crazy! You're all crazy!" She clapped her hands. "I love it! I love it! Let's get 'em!"

The captain clapped and clapped. Lisa did too. In a matter of seconds everybody was clapping and clapping and clapping.

The cameras faded out, the captain returned to the bridge, Tamara slipped into the tool room, Julian disappeared into his cabin, and thus began the new day.

The mouse clattered a couple of times on the metal desktop as Julian shook it reflexively to wake the slumbering computer. The screen brightened to its last open window—the handover report. He scanned the page with disinterest but lit up at the note about the leaking saltwater in-take. He reminded himself to definitely look into that today. He even went so far as to pull the small, weathered notebook from his khaki shorts pocket and added the task to his list. He scrolled through the rest of the items in the report, but nothing else jumped out at him.

An important part of engine maintenance is blowing them out occasion-ally, namely, speeding across open water for twenty minutes or so; however, the captain, for some reason or another, didn't adhere to this recommendation as often as she could, almost as if she were afraid to be at speed that something might break. Maybe she didn't trust the crew to be on deck and not get thrown into the drink. Whatever it was, she rarely opened up the throttle and tore off across the Sea of Cortez.

This day, however, was the exception. Tamara started up the engines, recorded the measurements on each of the gauges, let the diesel and oil and fluids circulate to life, and when the engines were sufficiently warmed, she radioed the bridge that they could take off whenever.

The Abbey started slow with the regular soft jolt experienced below which informed the engineers that they were indeed moving forward. Tamara continued with her routine tasks, monitoring the gauges, checking the oil level on the resting generator, on the generator in use, and on the gear boxes. Always checking engine oil. Her hands were on the hatchway wheel about to spin it open when she lost her balance over the blast from the throttle. The engines screamed. She quickly confirmed the gauges to make sure nothing had blown, then scrambled into the tool room. Julian was waiting inside.

"She finally took our advice, eh?" he said to the stunned Tamara.

"I almost forgot how quick this thing could move."

"What do you say we ride this one out up top?"

The two engineers sat beneath the fly deck's canopy, alone, and let the ocean air waft over them. Above deck the engines didn't scream, they growled a steady confident growl. Water sprayed away from the cut of the hull, and occasionally, with the right burst of wind, the saltine wetness landed on their shaded faces.

Tamara lifted her chin and breathed the moisture in. "That feels so good."

"Doesn't it," Julian echoed. He tried not to look at her breasts, snugged by her fitted Trident Legion shirt. He didn't dare look down for the chance he'd stare at her gentle, pale, legs revealed by the shorts she rarely wore, as she spent most of her time in coveralls, covered in grease.

All of a sudden, her hand grasped his and she pointed out to sea.

"Over there!" she shouted. She gripped his hand tighter. "Look over there! Look over there! Do you see? Do you see them?"

Julian didn't know what had her so frantic, he focused solely on her hand touching his. The ship quit its advance and slowed to a near drift. Any quicker a pull on the throttle and the engines would have been thrust into reverse.

"A pod of dolphins!" she said.

Julian squinted. At first, he didn't see anything. The swollen sea danced with reflecting light and appeared blue and pink and purple and green. Little white caps rolled now and again. He squinted harder.

"Holy cow!" he gasped in recognition.

The little white caps were not little white caps at all. They were the reentry splashes of hundreds of dolphins racing to meet the ship's path.

Tamara leaned in and hugged Julian's arm. She never let go of his hand.

"Look at you two lovebirds," the man said from the bridge's hatch.

Tamara pulled out of her embrace. She let go of Julian's hand. She rolled her eyes. "It's not like that, you arse. Did you see what's out there?"

Ed smirked. He winked at Julian. "That's what I came up here to tell you."

"You shouldn't have killed the engines so quick."

"That was the captain. We weren't sure how big the pod was and didn't want to risk anything."

"Except our ship?"

Ed stepped up onto the fly and stared out at the approaching pod. Without looking at Julian, he asked, "Hey, didn't you say something about a leak in the engine room?"

"I'm investigating."

"What leak?" Tamara asked surprised.

"One of the intakes," he said. "I'll show you after."

"As cool as the view is from up here, you might want to get down on the bow and hang over the ledge," Ed said. His face perked up with the recollection. "They'll bow ride and sing and cross over each other so close you can reach out and touch them."

"Really?" Julian asked.

"Really," Tamara said. "It's a riot."

As if trying to hear something delicate, Ed raised his ear and lopped his mouth slightly ajar. "Do you hear that?"

Julian listened then shook his head.

"I think I hear wedding bel—" But before he could finish his taunt, Tamara punched him in the shoulder. "Ow!" Ed rubbed his shoulder vigorously. "That hurt."

Tamara smiled. She blew on her knuckles like they were the barrel of a smoking gun. She flexed her fingers to examine her nails—of which she had none—and hummed a sigh. "Good," she said plainly.

There were already people on the bow. Everyone who was there held a camera aimed on the action, everyone except for either of the engineers. The ship gathered speed, not full throttle like they'd been travelling on route to the Vaquita refuge, but enough to keep the interest of the dolphins, who were fast upon the ship's trajectory.

In what appeared to be choreographed precision, the dolphins, common bottle nosed, breached the surface in a crescent arc and dove expertly into the water, each time building speed to achieve higher and longer leaps from the sea. One and then another, crisscrossing and taking the lead and falling behind and always moving forward, never colliding. These mammals gave all the indication of having a blast of a time in their autonomous marine lives.

A flurry of shutters clicked open and closed as lenses zoomed in and out trying to capture the perfect frame.

Julian, face aglow, turned to Tamara. He thought about squeezing her tight, then thought better of it, and instead simply said, "This is amazing."

She smiled. "They'll be here in second," she said. She knelt over the bow, then stretched out her legs so as to be laying over the side but counter-balanced enough on deck not to fall in with the steady bounce of the ship.

Julian fumbled to his knees and attempted to copy her pose, armpit resting on the gunwale, lower body extended behind. "This is not comfortable at all," he said, shifting and groaning to find the right position.

"You'll forget about it in a—"

A dolphin, wide as Julian and twice as long, exploded from the water and flew across the bow before completing its dive beneath the surface. Two other bottlenose came up from the side of the ship. Their tails flapped confidently as their beaks pressed ever forward held strong in stoic regard. One of them jumped, and in the flash of sun, no one would argue against the smile that crossed the mammals face.

"Get lower, get lower," Tamara urged. "I almost touched that one."

The two engineers reached as low as they could. The dolphins broke the surface, slipped back under, crossed each other, flapped their tails, and raced along the bow of the Edward Abbey. Their magnificent presence captivated everyone on deck. Words like beautiful, majestic, innocent, playful, cute, adorable, and superior, were freely exchanged among the crew.

Although neither Tamara or Julian could reach the smooth, oil slick skin of a single dolphin, they both continued to try. There was nothing but dolphins. Dolphins as far as they could see. The sound of their dashing through the wake, their cut from and to the sea, their song, words spoken in verse like poetry recited in a distant language, engulfed the ship.

And then they were gone.

Julian scanned the water, still hung over the ledge, smile glued to his face, eyes dilated, high.

Tamara righted herself on deck and leaned against the bow's gunwale. "Pretty awesome, don't you think?"

Julian arched back then collapsed contented beside her. "I could do that forever. How many do you think there were?"

"Hundreds, easily."

"And then they just disappeared."

"They're wonderful, aren't they?"

"Engineer, engineer, engineer," The broadband squelched from Tamara's pocket. Both her and Julian, the way they were seated, were staring at the bridge by default. She pulled the lanyard clipped to the radio and swung the device to her mouth.

"This is Engineer."

"We want open up the engines again, are we good to go?"

"Heading down below right now. We'll let you know in a minute, over."

In the tool room, Tamara stared at the task list tacked to the wall. On her finger, she spun a size 21-crescent wrench. She sucked on her bottom lip.

"Well aren't you going to check the gauges?"

Her forehead scrunched. "What?"

"The captain."

"No."

"What?"

"The engines are fine; I could have told her that from up there. I just like making them wait for an answer." She grinned. "Engineers run the ship, baby."

He chuckled. "Just call it in. I want to go look at that leak."

When both engines ran together, a wrench could fall on the metal grates and never be heard. It's why they were always turning up lost tools in the bilge whenever they drained it.

Julian tapped the side of his head, his temple. "I think we can spot it from here!" He attempted to be heard above the growl of the engines. Tamara shrugged.

He set his pocket size Maglite on the grate and knelt beside it. He removed the panel closest to the where the starboard saltwater intake was located beneath the engine. Water sloshed in the bilge as the ship accelerated. A droplet splashed above Julian's eye and he jerked away, palming his eye socket to wipe it clean. He thumbed the flashlight and shone the beam through the various manifolds and pipes. The light landed on the green pipe under question. He traced it back to the bulkhead. A steady stream flowed from the joint, precisely where Gilles had indicated in the handover report.

Julian hung his head. It was worse than he thought. Worse than he hoped. He rolled onto his side and signalled for Tamara to have a look. He trained the beam on the leaking pipe and waited for Tamara to say something.

Her mouth gaped.

In the tool room, Julian hung his ear defenders and then hung Tamara's pair.

"What are we going to do about that?" she asked. She wore a concerned look, face stricken, one Julian hadn't seen before; one completely devoid of confidence.

He bit his knuckles. "Well."

Tamara stared.

"It's probably a good thing you got the pump working, I guess." He pouted a smile but Tamara didn't reciprocate. She really did look worried. "We'll just fill a bunch of homer buckets and dump them overboard."

"We can't put that oily sludge in the water."

"I think there are exceptions."

"No way." She shook her head. "Even if the captain went for it, most of Lisa's deck crew would have a fit—they're true blue ideologues."

"Tamara," he said. "We're taking on water. The bilge is already higher than I've ever seen it. I'll put some more of that metal filler around it, another coat of sealant, but we have to get the bilge pumped so was can start keeping an eye on it, measuring and whatever."

"I don't know how you're going to get the stuff overboard in secret."

"You just get the pump set up. I'll run up and grab some buckets."

She looked annoyed. "Why didn't you look into this sooner, like, when you got the report?"

Julian shrugged and slipped out of the tool room.

Topside, he ran into Ed, who was down from the bridge and standing on the bow. The drone's giant Pelican case lay open on the deck. The media team were piecing together the blades.

"What's all this?" Julian asked.

Ed pointed ten o'clock off the bow. "See that black spot on the surface out there?"

Julian stared at what he thought Ed was pointing at. "Okay," he replied. "You think it's a panga?

"No, it doesn't look like a boat. Thinking maybe more like that whale we found all bloated and tangled in the net."

Julian shivered. The sour, rotting, bloated flesh of the Cachalote had embedded itself so firmly in the scent nerves of Julian's brain that he shivered at the recollection. "That was disgusting," he managed. Julian tried to focus his eyes on the floating object. "I thought we sunk it."

"We did."

"That'd be pretty bad if there was another one this close."

"Media's going to fly the drone over and take a look."

"So, we're stopping the ship again?"

"Just for a minute. We'll let them take off and then we'll stay on course to the refuge. If they turn up anything, we'll head over. No need to waste fuel, right?"

Julian untied the stack of homer buckets from the fire bunker.

"Find that leak?" Ed said.

"Mm-hmm."

"Have fun with that."

Julian pointed at the black spot, and in a tone of pure sincerity said, "Have fun with that."

Tamara knelt beside the Honda water pump and primed the motor. The intake and output hose lay beside each other on the grating. First, she connected the intake hose, verifying the arrow on the coupling to make sure, then she attached the output hose. Her foot held the pump steady as she reamed on the starter cable.

The engine rumbled awake and chugged in metronomic routine.

She was about to return to the tool crib when Julian stepped through with the buckets.

"What's going on up there?" She mouthed and thumbed in the direction of the engines, which had idled and revved and idled again under the captain's whim.

He set the buckets near the Honda pump and approached her. He lifted one of the cups protecting her ears.

"They're sending up the drone!" He shouted.

She jumped, and when she did, the cup snapped back around her ear.

"Jeeze!" she said, shaking her head and repositioning her ear defenders.

Julian's eyes popped in shock. He mouthed an apology. "So-rr-y," he said. And he was. He'd never done that before, lifting the ear defender off her head to say something, never really encroached any of her personal space deliberately before, only now with the chest incident, and the cheek kiss, and the hand grasp, and the arm hug, something had shifted somehow normalizing the impulse to pull the cup and get close enough to tell her something. Only, he managed to completely unromanticize the gesture, if there was ever even a way to romanticize it. She stared at him queerly, inspecting.

Finally, she nodded to the buckets. He pulled the stack apart, one at a time, and set them beside each other on the walkway. He positioned the output hose in the first bucket and signalled for the intake side to be dropped into the bilge.

Black sludge slurped up the hose, slurp-slurp-slurp. The nozzle bounced around inside the lip of the homer bucket. When they'd filled five buckets, Tamara switched the pump off. Julian craned his neck toward the hatch and both exited to the tool room.

"We're going to need more buckets," she said.

"Oh yeah, I'm thinking we could probably fill ten more with what's down there."

"So, how are we going to get this overboard without anybody noticing?"

Julian sighed. "We'll do it at sunset, or just after, how about during dinner when everybody's in the mess?"

"Dinner probably works best."

"I'll throw some absorbent pads on top for now. They'll soak up ninety percent of the gunk. As long as we're moving and the sun's set or setting, I figure we just dump them in our wake. Even if the pads miss some, at least nothing will pool around the hull. And if we cross it on our way back, it will look like another ship leaked it. God knows there are enough of those derelict boats around."

"Just for the record, I'm not on board with any of this. This is all on you, Chief."

As if cued, the radio squelched, interrupting the engineers.

"They're a needy bunch today, eh?" Julian commented, ignoring her recorded stance.

Chapter Thirteen: Shadow

The M/V Edward Abbey adjusted course and headed toward the black mass floating in the water. At first, the media team thought it was something beautiful. The early images the drone relayed back to the controller displayed the sun refracted in a halo around the prehistoric shell, its legs extended and coasting on the surface with its head reaching carving through the water. It was exactly what would collect 'likes' on the Trident Legion social feed. A campaign ordained by the Gods of Ocean Tides: an eighty-year-old Pacific green turtle following along with the conservation ship, in support of Milagro IV, in the rescue of the endangered Vaquita marina dolphin. The excitement grew and the video screen was passed about the crew. What are the chances, right? Such a rare find. Such beauty. Can you imagine? The operator resumed control and adjusted the camera angle. She brought the drone closer to the sea turtle. It's when everything became not alright—because it never was.

Cinched tight around the throat of the magnificent twelve-foot turtle was the unmistakable and universally hated aquatic green of gill net multi filament. The joy of spotting this elusive creature was shattered by the cold reality of another reckless murder at the hands of the immoral fishermen.

Ed tapped Julian on the shoulder. "We need you to take a look at the panga engine," he said. "Ben says it's having issues starting."

"When are you sending it out?"

Ed grinned. "Now."

"It's probably the fuel line," Julian said. "Don't worry, I'm on it."

Since the time he'd arrived on the Abbey, with zero experience as engineer, Julian had become intimately acquainted with all the different systems onboard the ship. The sewage system and its finicky poop chute sensor which when repairing was prudent to aim the L-joint away when forcing compressed air through; fuelling and how it required two people to confirm the levels when filling up, one at the pump and one inside, less the tanks exceed their capacity and flood the mess in diesel; the crane; the windlass; and all the electronics including the radar, which is remarkably complicated—but even that he knew the tweaks to bring it back online and resolve whatever the issue was—namely, turn it off and turn it back on again. Julian figured engineering was pretty much the study of systems and their supply chain. Look forward and roll it back. All those holier-than-thou true blue engineers could shove their pinky fingers up the L-joint of the poop chute sensor as far as he was concerned.

Comparably, the panga was a breeze. Ben stood at the crane's controls and pulled on the levers to swing the boom over the deck and lower the panga into the water. After it was tethered to the Abbey, Julian climbed down and began his investigation. He traced the fuel line from the tank to the outboard motor. Nothing appeared amiss. He checked the connector cables on the battery and then the ignition coil and switch. When he turned the key, all the lights lit up and all the needles on the miniature gauges flickered to life. He turned over the ignition, felt the starter trying, but still, the motor wouldn't take. Julian checked the fuel shutoff on the jerrycan.

"You're an idiot, Ben," Julian said.

Ben leaned on the stanchions above and pouted as if it couldn't possibly be his fault. "How am I an idiot? I did everything you just did."

"When was the last time you checked the fuel?"

"Every time I get in the thing. The gauge says three quarters."

Julian lifted the jerrycan. It appeared to float from its space near the transom and high above Julian's head. "Three quarters, huh?" He tapped the empty jerry on the side of the Abbey. The hollow echo inside the thick red plastic bounded up the hull.

"That's not my fault," he whined. "The gauge is obviously broken. Pass it up here."

The swell lifted the Abbey and settled the panga at different times. After a couple of tries, Ben finally grabbed the jerry from Julian and ventured down to the engine room to have it filled.

Just to make sure that the fuel was the only issue plaguing the little fishing boat, Julian continued his inspection. The panel below the steering wheel stayed secured by its opposing cotter pins. Julian removed them and peeked inside. He chuckled. A half-drank bottle of Sailor Jerry's greeted him from behind the steering column. Ben pretended he was the most pure of Trident Legion of all the crew. He even bragged a direct email correspondence with the mighty Saul Swatson, founder and Lord of the Trident Legion. Ben had been on the ship the longest and was therefor most senior, despite not being the bosun; and here, tucked away in his prized panga: obvious contraband. At least it wasn't Captain Morgan's.

Aside from the bottle, nothing appeared amiss to Julian. He replaced the panel and was securing the second cotter pin when Ben returned with the fuel jerry. The colour of his face stole away when he spotted Julian crouched where he was. He didn't say anything.

Julian turned around and reached for the jerry. "Everything looks good down here," he smiled. "Probably just the fuel."

Ben composed himself. "So, I guess—do you have any—that gauge, huh?"

Julian chuckled but otherwise didn't let on that he saw anything. To each their own. "I'll look into it. Besides that you're good to go." He climbed the accommodation ladder. "What are you guys going to do with that turtle?"

"Same as what we do with the other nets, measure, record, snap some pictures. Cut that noose from around its neck."

"I don't know how you guys handle all these dead things all day."

"I don't know how you handle all the grease and fumes all day."

Julian nodded. "Hmm. Well, good luck and all."

Eyes trained on the drone screen Ed asked, "Fix it?"

Julian peered over Ed's shoulder. "Are those herring gulls perched on the shell?"

"Catching a ride, I guess."

An hour earlier and all the crew had been elated by the appearance of the mega-pod, their playful antics, their Cetacean way of trying to communicate. The world had become beautiful again, they were reinvigorated, they were ready to do what they were patrolling the Sea of Cortez ready to do.

And now this. Death.

On the panga were Ben, the media team, and Rodriguez. Even as they approached the giant turtle, they couldn't believe it had died. The mammoth shell arced out of the water and carried with it an air of prominence, of wisdom, of compassion, the way an old man at the end of his life reminiscent of his wife, his children grown, the grand kids, and how lying there on the hospital bed about to expel his last breath, he's contented by everything he's had—the turtle carried that kind of esteem.

As they neared the prehistoric creature, they quickly understood that this was not a peaceful death. This was murder, and with it, all the intimation associated with a violent crime. The scene was heavy with the pungent scent of warm flesh becoming cold, of bird stool baked onto its exoskeleton, of anal seepage and thick copper blood. Surprisingly, it was not nearly as bad as the rotting whale found the previous month, however, distinct in its own terror to become embedded in the nasal passages of each of the crew on board the tiny panga fishing boat.

Ben positioned the panga near the head of the giant creature. Its eyelids were heavy and closed. Its chin rested on the surface as if during its final breaths it reached for the sun one last time. The green noose cut into the leather skin so tight that the neck had folded over. The netting, which ultimately tore free from the rest which remained submerged somewhere in the deep, hung across its left flipper.

"Rody," Ben said. "You hook the net with the gripper and I'll cut it free."

The media crew clicked their camera's over and over again. The snapping shutters took on a funeral march cadence.

Rodriguez leaned over the edge of the panga, gripper in hand, and set it gently on the netted flipper. He hooked the net and pulled the panga nearly on top of the creature. Ben started to work the noose.

A red spurt, thick as spidering wine, streamed from the turtle's neck. In seconds, there was a river of ancient blood flowing out to sea, the current promising to carry the red thundercloud cloud as far as there remained blood to offer.

"What'd you do?" Rodriguez asked in horror. He held fast the net he'd retrieved.

"It was just a little nick, man." Ben shook his head. He'd reached over to cut the net free when a small swell took him off line ever so slight. The cut must have been enough to release the pressure of all the years of built up prestige.

"That's unbelievable."

"Well," Rodriguez said. He pointed overhead to the steady z-hum of the drone above. "They're going to believe it alright." A cackle escaped his realization. "Bad as it is, it's going to open up a lot of wallets."

The two media people had already decided as much. Ben noticed them nodding along.

"Maybe if we spun it around a couple times," he started to suggest but media was already there.

"We can get the blood to spiral spread, make it look deathly starcrossed."

So, that's what they did. Ben and Rodriguez slowly pivoted the animal three hundred and sixty degrees. The blood continued to pour from the trachea and drifted like ripples from the shell. Ben steered the boat away before the blood latched onto the hull and became pulled along with it.

The drone descended and panned around. From the Abbey, Ed and Julian watched the feed first-hand. The panga and the four crew it carried had anchored two boat-lengths from the creature. They posed horror stricken, hands cupping their eyes in the direction of the bloody mess. Aquamarine water separated the white boat and the red spectacle. The turtle, easily discernibly from above, floated on the surface, arms and legs spread, head extended—the glare of the sun drawing a halo amidst it all.

From the side, however, and wafting like the smoke of a white rabbit camp fire, a deep royal red hung in layers. The money shot.

"Alright, panga team," Ed said into the broadband. "You can wrap it up now and bring it in."

"Anything else we're supposed to do with this?"

"As long as you retrieved the net, that's all you can do."

The radio quieted to general static.

Port side, the faint whiz of the drone approached. One of the crew stood knees bent and arms reaching straight over head as the controller positioned the drone within reach. "Got it!" he said, gripping the skids with both hands.

The controller killed the motors and the oceanic breeze assumed primacy.

Chapter Fourteen: Plunge

The engineers sat quietly on the fly deck. The sky turned pastel with the setting of the sun. Along the horizon held blue, topped with a soft pink which rose into a shade of orange dotted by the clouds. Lazy ripples con- stituted the wake from the Abbey and reflected the sky in disappearing swells of turquoise and maroon. The engines hummed along and whoever commanded the ship from the bridge was silent in the captain's chair. The rest of the crew had congregated in the mess to eat dinner after what had become a Six Flags kind of a day. Though everybody refused to admit it, an air of apprehension had usurped the crew. Morale had plummeted and the thought of continuing to the objective at the edge of the Vaquita refuge had lost its appeal.

"It almost looks like oil," Tamara said, as she stared at the mixing sur- face behind the wake.

Julian nodded. He bit his lip, touched his hand to his mouth then bit a knuckle. "Well," he said, turning to face Tamara. "In risk of all—" He placed his fingertips on her cheek and leaned in.

For a moment neither engineer moved. Their lips were pressed to- gether but not quite kissing. Embarrassed, Julian was about to pull away when Tamara mouthed his lip gently. Then it began. They continued locked like this until the sun completely settled. When they let go a soft- ness enveloped both of their faces and for a moment neither him nor Tamara said a word.

The engines purred. The ocean swell slapped the hull in consistent ap- plause. The first stars appeared overhead. The two engineers inched their fingers together until they were holding hands.

"Don't break my heart," Tamara whispered, head nestled into his shoulder.

Julian squeezed her hand. After a brief silence, he asked, "Do you want to go below and I'll pull the buckets up through the hatch?"

She let go of him, pulling herself erect. "What?" she said, eyebrows scrunched. "Oh," she said, remembering the buckets. "That." Tamara hopped up from the bench and slid down the ladder. At the bottom, she said, "FYI. You're not very good at the romantic bit."

Julian opened the hatch separating the engine room from the aft-deck, separating the engine room and the starlit sky, and laid it flat on the surface. Its spring lock snapped into its housing, silent only for the grind of the engines now stealing into the night. Moving urgently but without haste, Julian secured a carabiner to the end of a rope and lowered it through the passageway. Tamara clipped the carabiner around the wire handle of one of the buckets and removed the floating absorbent pad from on top.

"I didn't believe it when you said so, but this thing did a pretty good job," she said.

Julian hauled on the rope until he could reach the handle for himself and pulled it up the rest of the way. With a quick look over his shoulder to make sure nobody had surfaced from below, he shuffled the slopping bucket to the stern of the ship. The ocean easily digested the once oily water into the Abbey's wake. Him and Tamara repeated this sequence until all five buckets were empty.

Before he closed the hatch, she called up to him. "Do you want to start the pump again?"

He thought about it for a moment. No was his first reaction, but they had to take advantage of the darkness. He agreed in the affirmative and away they went. The absorbent pads wouldn't have enough time to soak up all the sludge particles, but, Julian rationalized, fixing the leak was first priority—it really was a matter of survival.

They'd filled and dumped five more buckets and were tidying up the engine room when Ed entered. He wore the largest ear defenders in the tool room, the yellow reject pair, which for some reason always made the wearer look like Mickey Mouse. He'd also managed to procure the thickest pair of safety glasses. All he needed was a clipboard in hand and he'd be complete in his corporate stooge attire—out of place as a sore thumb down there. Both Julian and Tamara burst out laughing when they saw him.

He shouted something over the engines. Julian didn't even try to hear him. He nodded to Tamara to join him in the tool room, then led Ed out.

"You look like a goof," Julian teased.

"I don't know how you guys work in there."

"Guy and girl," Tamara said in a tone that made it impossible to tell if she were kidding or not.

Julian saved Ed the trouble and asked him what he'd come down for.

"There's a boat on the radar where the target is supposed to be."

"One of the poachers retrieving the net?" Tamara asked.

"Looks like it," Ed said. "It's not PROFEPA or the navy, that's for sure. Captain already called both."

"So, what's the plan?" Julian asked. His face tightened and his lips pursed as he thought about the last time they'd come up against a poacher at a targeted site—the night the young man slipped into the ocean and didn't come out breathing.

"Repeat of last time?" Tamara asked as if she were reading Julian's mind.

Ed stared her in the eyes. "No," he said flatly, then shifted his attention to Julian. "No," he repeated. "That was a worse-case scenario, that became the worst-case scenario. It won't happen again. The captain's not going to risk anything like that—I promise."

Julian stroked his mouth with open hand. After a minute, he asked, "What do you need us to do?"

Chapter Fifteen: Contact

Splashes of swell jumped over the bow as the captain increased the throttle. Julian and Tamara found themselves returned to the fly deck on special assignment from Ed.

The snap-buttons snapped open as Julian pulled the canvas cover protecting the 30,000-lumen spotlight. Tamara folded it, set the cover aside, then reached for the toggle switch. Julian slapped her hand away.

"Ouch!" she cried.

He hadn't hit her hand hard, but the way she reacted, he wished he hadn't slapped her hand like that at all. Julian was a little tense over their plan of attack.

"Sorry," he said. "It works, I know it does. I tested it during my inspection earlier."

"You didn't need to smack my hand."

"You were going to give away our position," he whined.

"As if they can't hear us already." She pointed at the mast. "Or see our running lights." The bow, the port and starboard side, the bridge, and the mast were all lit up. Tamara rubbed the top of her hand and growled.

"Would you feel better if I let you slap me back?" He said, offering the top of his hand as recompense.

"Matter-a-fact I would," she said, but instead of accepting his offered hand, she wound up and set her open palm across Julian's cheek.

"Ow!" he cried. "That was a smack."

"Hmm," she said with an air of indifference, then smiled contently. "I guess you shouldn't hit a woman."

"Engineer, this is Bridge," the radio crackled, though whoever was speaking could be heard through the open hatch of the bridge.

The two school-children flirts looked at each other, then to the radio, then to the open doorway.

The voice transmission continued, this time without the radio. "Are you two going to quit fooling around or should I send you back to your hole?" It was the captain.

Julian mouthed, What the heck? Rarely did she address the engineers so condescendingly. Tamara shrugged.

"We're good, Captain," Julian said flatly.

"The spotlight doesn't leave the panga."

"Just say when," Julian said.

"Do you have a pair of binoculars up there?"

Tamara mouthed a sassy copy-cat of her words, Do you have a pair of binoculars up there? and waved the binoculars in Julian's face.

"Yes, Captain," he replied, eyes begging Tamara to knock it off.

"Then light them up."

"Roger that," he said and flicked the switch.

It took a minute for Julian to place the beam on the panga. He scanned the water running z-patterns like he'd seen the night of the man overboard. With the verbal directives of the captain, he settled on the small boat anchored on the edge of the protected area.

There were no markers indicating where the Vaquita refuge began, however, trawlers didn't venture this far west and all the locals were acutely aware that fishing out here would provoke immediate suspicion. Dropping nets was basically suicide.

Under the glare of the spotlight, the two rainwear-clad fishermen worked steadily to retrieve the catch from the net. They didn't look up or acknowledge the Abbey.

The captain slammed her hand on the chart table. "Do they want what happened last time?"

Julian kept the spotlight trained on the panga. Tamara spied what she could through the binoculars and reported her findings. The two fisher-men working on the net wore yellow jackets and black slush-pants. One fisherman remained at the wheelhouse of the tiny boat. His mouth moved speaking something to the others, but being spoken in Spanish and as far away as the Abbey still was to their position, it was impossible for Tamara to make out what was being said. It wasn't until after noting their fashion and that despite their not acknowledging the Abbey's proximity even though the ship's approach was obvious, how they appeared calm and in casual conversation, that Tamara noticed something out of place. Each of the men wore black balaclavas. An eye hole for each eye and an opening for the mouth.

"That's odd," she said.

"What do you want us to do, Captain?" Ed asked.

She drummed the chart table, pinky to pointer, as she deliberated the next move. It was the exact fear which gripped Julian.

"We maintain course," the captain said.

"Captain—" Julian started in a tone that threatened insubordination.

Before he could finish his thought, Tamara interrupted. "I think they're getting ready to shoot at us—"

Julian stared into the beam lighting up the boat. He could see that the fisherman had stopped retrieving the net, but he couldn't make out what sparked Tamara's concern.

"They look like slingshots—" she said.

"Slingshots?" Ed remarked.

The first projectile crashed through the glass above the depth finder at the first mates chair. The leaded object thudded to the floor and rolled with the steady breath of the ship. The hole whistled like a battle cry at dawn.

The captain flicked on the red nightlights of the bridge. She and Ed looked for whatever it was that had come crashing though.

Held against the light between Ed's thumb and middle finger, the unmistakable lead weight used to anchor the line of a gill net. The Abbey housed buckets of these balls, back of the ship, near the Parley bags. They were stored there in wait of their sister ship to rendezvous in order to pass them off and have them melted into dive belt-weights stamped with the trademark Trident Legion skull and cross bones as fundraiser swag.

A second lead ball cracked the fire lockers below.

"They keep shooting, Captain!" Tamara hollered. Her and Julian remained steadfast at their post, exposed on the fly deck. He kept the light trained. She kept eyes on.

The captain picked up her own binoculars and focused through the lenses. It's when the next lead ball struck.

Julian groaned.

The little projectile crashed through the protective glass of the spotlight and smashed the lumen bulb. The mosaic of shards and sparks caused him to stumble back and in stumbling, Julian knocked his head off the overhead beam. He hunched over and gripped his skull.

"Are you hit?" Ed hollered.

"No," Julian whimpered. "Just banged my head is all. But they took out the spotlight."

"Captain," Tamara said with hesitation in her voice. "Captain it looks like they're lighting something."

Apparently, the captain had observed the same thing because before Tamara could express her concern, the Abbey had pitched forward. Julian stumbled back from his already unstable stance and knocked his head against the same beam.

"Argh!" he growled.

Tamara knelt to steady herself. She reached out for Julian and held his head over his own gripping hand.

"Least it wasn't a rock to the eye," she said playfully.

He didn't speak.

Under the steering of the captain, the Abbey sped toward the lone fishing boat at the edge of the Vaquita refuge. If the situation wasn't so life threatening, the manoeuvre would have appeared choreographed like a stunt scene in a movie. The fisherman behind the wheelhouse had the engine ready and when the Abbey was only its own ship-length away, one of the men in the yellow rainwear and black slush-pants launched the flaming bottle into the air. The captain swung the wheel port side as the driver of the panga threw the throttle forward on his own boat. The Molotov bottle struck the Abbey's hull and exploded into a thick lava-like flame, clinging to the ship. The little boat shot off in the opposite direction.

The captain activated the alarm.

"Ed, Julian!" the captain yelled. "Get the fire team dressed and put water on that flame."

The two men flew down the ladder; Julian to the engine room, Ed to round up the others. They rendezvoused at the fire lockers and began dressing. Julian activated the water pumps and joined Ed on the bow. The hoses were already laid out on the deck. Rodriguez and Tawd were awaiting instruction. It was thirty seconds for Julian to catch up, but in that short moment, the flame had ignited several of the greased stanchions.

"Tell me when!" Rodriguez yelled.

Ed picked up the nozzle, aimed it at the creeping flame, and yelled, "Now!"

If not for Julian's hand supporting Ed's shoulder, Ed would have been thrown backward when he flipped the lever, the hose held that much pressure. Water hissed from the nozzle as Ed steadied his aim. Julian maintained his supporting position, pushing on Ed to keep him upright. Complementing the effort, Tawd unloaded a pressurized multi-purpose extinguisher good for suppressing fuel induced fires. A-B-C class, a pale yellow powder you do not want to get in your eyes or mouth. He sprayed the chemical over all the subdomain fires: the lifelines, the bubbling deck, the stanchions.

The fire wouldn't quit though. Tawd smacked Julian's back. "This isn't working," he said. "Someone's got to lean over the hull and aim down below."

Tawd was right. Each of the crew on deck knew it, too. But what everybody also knew that it was impossible to lean over the side of the ship with the hose pumping all that water. It was like a steel pipe when deployed, and as everybody is well aware, steel does not bend.

As quick as the water had shot through the hose, when Ed threw the lever forward, it stopped.

"Rody!" Ed yelled. "Get the other extinguishers up here." He picked up his radio and called the captain. "We need you to kill the engines, I can't have anybody over the side while we're moving."

The captain acknowledged by slamming the throttle into near reverse. A pressure alarm in the engine room blared.

The clanging of steel bounded across the deck as Rodriguez returned, dragging the extinguishers.

"Julian, you're with me. Tawd, you're up front. Keep the extinguisher deck side, get low, and cover as much of the hull as you can."

"What do you want me to do?" Rodriguez asked in timid apprehension.

"You get the life ring ready. If one of us does go over, it's a repeat of last time, except it will be one of us that isn't going home."

Fear shone white on Rodriguez's dark face. He started detaching the life rings. Tawd, Julian, and Ed assumed their positions, knelt on the deck to ensure the extinguishers remained this side of the life lines, and aimed their tiny black nozzles at the smouldering flame.

When the three extinguishers had sputtered out, all of the flaming napalm concoction had been smothered. They fell against the bulkhead and breathed for the first time since the fire began. Sweat poured from each of their fire-retardant face coverings, balaclava's in their own rights.

"This feels like a lot like war," Tawd reflected. "I love it."

Julian wiped his brow, unVelcroed the fire jacket from around his neck and laid his extinguisher by his side. "That could have been very, very bad," he said, surprisingly calm.

"Bad?" Ed said, obviously shocked. "This is bad. This whole thing is bad. Don't they know they're playing with people's lives?"

It wasn't a question for anyone, so Julian didn't answer, but he was thinking and what he thought was, Isn't what we're doing playing with theirs?

The captain called Ed to the bridge. Ed told the guys to gear down and put the expelled extinguishers in the lockup to be refilled when they get back to harbour.

"Someone's going to have to monitor this mess for a flareup," Julian said.

"Rody," Ed said. "You're first on watch. I'm going to see what the captain wants."

Chapter Sixteen: Regroup

The last of the hose was mounted and the security bar latched in place. Ed reappeared on the deck. "Maybe we shouldn't put that away," he said.

Bodies lined up behind him, each wearing an inflatable PFD, and each with a head lamp strapped to their forehead. Red lights flicked off and on as anxious fingers toggled with the settings.

"What's going on?" Tawd asked.

Rodriguez and Julian nodded in bewilderment.

In the distance, a tiny white light bobbed at sea. Beside it, another, and beside that, another. Equally spaced all around the ship little white lights flickered a threatening presence.

"The radar has a dozen boats moving in on our position," Ed said.

Ben and his panga team tightened the straps on the cradle where the panga was stored behind the crane. Lisa gave tasks to each of the crew about the immediate lock down. Even the media personnel assisted in barring the accommodation ladders slung on the side of the ship. Several other crew removed the ladders which connected the deck and bridge. The buckets of lead were dragged along the weathered and now slick deck and set in strategic positions several metres apart. A sharp whiz fractured the air behind Julian. He jumped. The drone spun off into the darkness, visible only by its blinking green and red lights alternating beneath the propellers.

"This is insane," Julian said.

"This is Trident Legion," Ed stated, his confidence seemingly renewed by whatever pep talk he received on the bridge. "This isn't the first time, and won't be the last."

"So, we're going to chuck lead at fisherman—fisherman who just blasted our ship with a Molotov cocktail? This isn't a game, Ed."

A solid thump pounded the deck. Tawd busied himself unrolling the fire hose they'd just put away. He reconnected it to the fire pumps and attached the nozzle. He stood at the ready, braced against flagpole of the fluttering pirate flag. The same place Tamara and Julian had laid reaching for the bow riding dolphins.

"It was never a game, Julian." Tawd hollered from his attack position. "Buck up or buck off."

"So, your plan is to blast them out of the water with the hose?" Julian groaned. "They'll drown."

"They just tried to sink us, Chief. What would have happened if we didn't get the fire put out? Survival of the fittest."

"This is nuts," Julian said.

"Captain needs you in the engine room, anyway," Ed said. "Tamara's already down there."

Julian fumed at the ears. He burst through the tool room door with fists clenched. He paced the tiny space. The entire campaign had been one blunder after another and now the captain wanted to go to war with the locals. He could already picture another death at the hands of their beloved Legion. A death buried under a mountain of propaganda. All the altruistic, meticulously crafted images sold to the highest bidder. Enough already. He wouldn't have any part of it. Get Tamara and go. Yes. As soon as they returned to shore, they would just walk off the ship and never look back. Done. No problem.

He grabbed his ear and eye protection and hurried into the engine room to exhort his adhoc plan to Tamara—but all the rage evaporated when he saw two feminine legs kicking and squirming from beneath the starboard engine. Julian lost no time sidling up to Tamara and trying to get an eye on what she was doing.

Water and sludge sloshed at the bulkhead beneath the grated gangway. The level it was at should have been impossible considering they'd only just dumped those near dozen buckets overboard. His eyes popped when he realized the seal might have finally gave way.

A hand reached back from under the engine. Tamara carefully pulled herself from underneath. She nodded for Julian to look, passed him the flashlight, then wiped her hands on her overalls. The steady stream of water from the intake pipe was a Bronx street fire hydrant spraying. The cone of water spewed from the cracked seal with relentless pressure. Still, at least the seal hung on. Whatever needed to be done needed to be done quick.

Julian wheeled the engine hatch closed behind him. He stood dumbly at the tool room entrance. "We need that engine off," he said.

"I don't know how many times I've told her not to throw the throttle back like that."

"If we kill the engine, it will stop pulling water and we have a better chance of getting it sealed."

"Aren't the poachers closing in?"

Julian forgot all about the advancing pangas. All the issues running circles in his head. Those twelve little assaulters with overblown engines toting vengeful fishermen would soon be on them. If the Abbey dropped an engine and gave up all that power, the pangas could keep up with them no problem, and—he picked up the radio and called the bridge.

"Captain," he said. No response. "Captain," he said again.

Tamara shook her head, then flinched into a cower.

The radio exploded against the shelving. Tiny plastic shards bounced around the room. Julian huffed.

"Jesus," Tamara hissed. "What's gotten into you?"

He turned his back on her and rubbed his face heavily. Tamara rested a hand on his shoulder which he shrugged off.

"This is all messed up," he said. "I'm not even an engineer."

Tamara snorted, then she chuckled. She removed her hand then forced a few laughs. He twisted his face and looked at her.

"Are you finished?" she said, snapping short her guffaw.

"What?"

"Your poor little me speech." She clenched her fists and raised them to the corners of her eyes. She puffed out her lips and started twisting her wrists and whining like a schoolyard bully taunting a sissy on the playground. "I'm not even an engineer," she mocked. "I want to go home. I want my mommy."

Julian straitened up. He glared.

"You think I'm an engineer?" Tamara scolded. "You think Ed's a first mate? The only people on this ship who's actually what their job description implies are the captain and the cook."

She had a point. Somewhere deep in Julian's mind he knew Tamara wasn't an engineer, that she only liked getting dirty in the engine room; just like somewhere in there he knew Ed wasn't really a first mate. None of them were actually anything but play acting—except for media. And like a kid in the wrong, he threw a haymaker, even though he knew he was beat.

"The media people are their job descriptions."

Tamara threw her radio at him.

Not Julian, but his reflex, caught it with both hands.

"Don't break this one," she said coldly. She pushed passed him and into the mess.

Julian repeated his call to the bridge. He explained the situation.

"Are you really advising me to cut our power in half while we're under attack?" the captain said. Her glare radiated through the receiver.

"Captain," Julian began, hesitantly. "We're taking on water." He paused. "We'll sink ourselves if we keep it up." He bit his lip.

"And why didn't you fix this before?"

Julian cocked his head. His face unnerved. He didn't know she knew about the handover report.

"We're not killing the starboard engine. Go do your job and sort it out."

Chapter Seventeen: Offensive

The shots ambushed the Abbey. Rodriguez worked from his knees and was pouring Ben's acid mixture in a glass milk jug when a leaded weight hissed by his ear and crashed into the exhaust vents.

"Chinga!" he chirped as he ducked his head very, very late.

Ben steadied the bottle Rodriguez held tipped at a dangerous angle.

"Don't spill that stuff on yourself Rody, it burns."

"They shot at me!"

Ben's surveyed the sea. "Well," he said, calmly. "I guess we better hurry up."

The media team assumed their position on the fly deck. One of them removed the canvas cover on the starboard spot light and powered it up. The other kept the camcorder trained on the action. From the fly, it's a 360-degree view, up and down and all around, perfect for covering all the angles, a vantage point snipers have wet dreams about.

The captain kept the Abbey wheeled tight to the left at a low speed drawing concentric circles in the water. Regardless her apparent apprehension, she was prepared to kick the ship into high gear and shoot off across the sea if the situation dictated.

Several of the deck crew chucked handfuls of weights toward the enemy pangas.

"Don't waste those when they're still that far out," Lisa said. "They'll be on us soon enough."

Tawd hollered from the bow. "Lisa, twist that valve open, will ya? They're in range for me." He steadied up against the flag pole and aimed the nozzle at the nearby fisherman. Lisa worked the fire hose wheel until it stopped turning.

The fisherman could very well have been the same ones the Trident Legion had first encountered. Each wore a yellow rain jacket too large for their small Mexican figures, black wader overalls, and black balaclavas. The man standing behind the wheelhouse had his balaclava rolled up to his forehead, face exposed as if to boast his lack of fear; as if to exemplify his courage. And he didn't look scared, chest proud puffed like Superman, death stare glaring in Tawd's direction, the man looked like he had nothing to lose. He probably didn't.

Two of his comrades pulled back on their slingshots and steadied their aim. At the same exact moment, beneath the Abbey, saltwater was being sucked up, run through the engine room pumps, elbowed up to the deck, and pressurized behind Tawd's nozzle. He throttled the lever and discharged a blast of water straight into the sea only two feet ahead of the advancing panga.

"A near miss!" Tawd complained above the crash of water. He interrupted the flow and ceased firing.

The water remained damned in the hose waiting another turn. The pangas circled opposite the Abbey, zigzagging each other like the dolphins from earlier in the day. A panga would rush in, lob their lead loads at the 110-ft Coast Guard Cutter, then dash out of reach from Tawd's fire hose.

The loud speaker squelched, commanding the attention of everybody on deck. "Hold on to something!" the captain ordered. "I'm swinging her starboard."

The crew dashed to grab hold of any object that was bolted to the deck. Rodriguez hugged the crane. Others wove their arms through the life lines. Everybody got low.

"This is your chance Tawd." The captain added. And with that, she swung the wheel hard right. Mugs crashed off their shelf in the mess. In Julian's tool room, parts were ejected from their bins and clattered on the floor. A spray-wall of saltwater rose over the bow as the Abbey cut through its own wake in a figure-eight.

This sporadic change of course surprised the fisherman and several nearly collided with each another while they scrambled to escape being crushed by the monstrous steel hull of the Edward Abbey. The fishermen were caught off guard, but not Tawd. When the captain swung the wheel hard right and the rest of the crew were hunkered down to embrace the sharp slice through the sea, Tawd bolstered his position on the bow. He leaned heavily into the flag pole. He wedged his foot between a brace in the bulkhead and a nub on the deck. His other foot he anchored to the pole by twisting his shin over the triangle and hooking the pole with his instep. He wasn't going anywhere. When the captain swung the ship's wheel hard right Tawd was grounded as a giant. He rose with the bow as the ship cut through its own wake and the wall of sea crashed all around. He slapped the lever open again.

A blast of icy ocean erupted from the nozzle, sliced the blinding sea wall, and exploded from whence it came—a laser from the Abbey's bow.

As the pangas struggled to regain their choreographed attack on the Abbey's quick change of direction, the fire hose unloaded its inexhaustible supply of ammunition. The two boat's trying to escape the Abbey's wake found themselves a metre away from the new threat. Both wheelhouse captains spun their wheels, one port, the other starboard and whipped around like a tracked tank on a dime. An explosive crack pierced the air above the whine of the full throttled panga engines, above the growl of the Abbey's twin diesels, above the fire pumps and streaming water. It was like a bullet shot over the head. Even the captain heard the snap from the bridge.

"Locate the strike!" the captain commanded over the loudspeaker.

Tawd flicked the lever off and killed the stream of water.

The captain maintained the ships trajectory.

After several minutes, Lisa reported to the bridge. "There's no damage down here and all the crew is accounted for."

Four pangas appeared to be regrouping at the spot the captain had manoeuvred the ship opposite. The captain, Lisa, and Ed stared on in wonderment, but it was Lisa who first noticed the smoke. "They're not regrouping," she offered. "I think—" She stared harder over the water. "I think two of them crashed. It looks like smoke rising from the back of those two pangas in the middle." She pointed.

Tawd cheered from the bow. "First try Tawd, baby!"

The drone hovered above the suspected crash site. It wasn't long before media confirmed what Lisa had guessed. When the two boats parried to avoid the spray from the fire hose, the propellers clipped each other.

"Two down, ten to go," Ed said.

The captained maintained the circular course and were coming upon the downed vessels.

Ben passed out the bottles that he and Rodriguez had filled with acid.

"Throw them hard enough so they shatter," Ben instructed. "If they manage to catch them and throw them back we're going to have quite the mess on our hands."

Each pair of eyes glazed with murder. It was a longing buttressed by all the carcasses retrieved from the abandoned gill nets. It was all the ancient animals discovered bloated and rotting snared in fragments of multi filament. It was the labour in pulling the kilometres of netting and packaging it up for Adidas. The angle of repose refused to hold any longer and came crashing down with acidic missiles.

A grunt escaped Ben's throat as he launched a Snapple bottle brimmed with his mixture at the first panga in striking distance. The fishermen on board the targeted boat spoke in rapid gestures assessing the damage while loosely keeping an eye on the approaching Abbey. One of them tossed a tow rope to the driver of the downed boat and if he hadn't looked over his shoulder in a cursory glance would have been levelled by Ben's whipped bottle. He ducked just in time for the glass to swoosh by his head and shatter in the hull of the panga.

"Like that, baby!" Ben yelled.

Hoo-yips and hollers echoed around the ship.

Curses and lead were fired back. Several of the fisherman loaded their slingshots and returned fire. A windowpane on the bridge was the first casualty of this counter-attack. The glass shattered inside and out raining tiny shards on the crew below.

"Hit them again," the loud speak blared.

Rodriguez lined up like a pitcher on his mound, threw his arm back, and released his bottle at the pangas. The fishermen were ready and easily escaped injury. Still, the bottle landed on target and shattered into the hull of the rescuing boat.

"There you go, Rody—" Ben started to praise.

A lead ball snapped by and struck Rodriguez. He fell immediately, gasping, and holding his chest.

Ben rushed to his side. "We need a medic up here!" He laid a hand on Rodriguez's shoulder and spoke softly. "You hit 'em Rod, you hit 'em good."

Rodriguez spoke only in moans. Ben scanned his body, starting at the head, looking for blood. There was none. Rodriguez wheezed as he breathed.

"I think—" he whispered. "It feels like—"

He sounded like a kid who'd winded himself falling off the monkey bars and Ben told him so.

"You sound like you got the wind knocked out of you, kid," Ben said.

Ed responded to Ben's plea for a medic and was standing above the two hunched over men. "I'll bring him below." He faced Rodriguez and chuckled. "People are going to start whispering things about us if we keep disappearing alone like this."

A pained cough was all Rodriguez could offer. Ed and Ben helped him to his feet.

Lead balls continued to pelt the Abbey. The two boats involved in the crash were secured to tow lines and attached to their sister pangas. Lisa crouched beside Ben to take cover.

"Why isn't anything happening?" she asked.

"It will happen," Ben assured. "All their splashing about must have sloshed the acid around. It will take. Give it a minute." He squinted at the four boats about to retreat.

Tawd continued his focused efforts from the bow ensuring none of the other pangas came too close. All the attackers appeared to have lost steam and were no longer as daring as their initial assault warranted them to be.

Ben continued. "I'm pretty sure the towed boat on the left and the towing boat on the right were the ones that got hit," he said.

Lisa stared, waiting for something, uncertain what to look for, only that Ben was certain something would indeed happen.

First there were screams. Then dancing, or what looked like dancing, by the crew in the towed boat on the left, and like Ben had predicted, in the towing boat on the right. Smoke rose from their hulls. The crews scrambled to their furthest gunwales, shoving one another, trying to get as far away from the smouldering mess as possible.

The wheelhouse captains picked up their radios and screamed urgently into their mouthpieces.

A whine of outboard motors sounded their retreat from the assault on the Abbey. The pangas hurried to their friends in need. It was an impromptu ceasefire as all the combatants were engaged in rescue—or suspended disbelief.

The fisherman hurried to pull their comrades from the inflicted vessels into their own boats. Everybody on deck the Abbey stood bewildered, imagining what the acid could be doing to cause such a commotion.

"Lisa!" Tawd yelled. "I can take them all, just need the captain to swing the ship over a bit. I'll be a sniper picking off soldiers trying to drag their injured buddies back behind cover." He laughed. "Put me in coach!"

She didn't hesitate. It was blood lust of the most primal initiative. Lisa radioed the captain, equally ravenous, who positioned the Abbey on the heels of the wounded pangas.

Like Julian ran Z patterns with the spotlight, Tawd steadied his pressurized assault on the stunned fishermen. Across the bow he aimed the spray, then cut diagonal striking two others. Across again. Giant Z's of angry water flooded the desperate panga teams. One by one their engines whined to escape the spray. It was only the original four which struggled to get away. Both towed boats filled with water. One of the towers smouldered under the burning acid.

An air horn blared from the acid inflicted vessel. One of the early escapees u-turned and sidled the troubled boat. The crew steadied themselves to pull the fisherman into their panga then sped off again, leaving their own boats behind.

The towed boat filled up first and slowly sunk below the water line. Its rope tightening and pulled at the stern of the abandoned acid riddled vessel. Tawd kept the hose aimed and filled it enough for it to quit resisting the tug of the sunken one. When the tip of the bow vanished below the surface cheers were all that could be heard for nautical miles.

"Did you see how fast those cowards ran?" someone offered.

Tawd grinned. "We can probably kill the valve, Lisa," he said. "I don't think they're coming back anytime soon."

Chapter Eighteen: Reprieve

Julian scoured the shelves in search of something to seal the leak. He dug through each milk crate and pulled out tube after tube of caulking. He found wood glue and metal filler and a can of sealant. These last two, he set in a tub, alongside a rag and a flashlight. "Go do your job and sort it out," he whined to himself as he geared up to do some patchwork under the starboard engine.

On the gangway between both roaring engines, Julian knelt, removed a grate, and stepped below. Water had already begun to fill the bilge and would keep doing so if the cracked elbow joint wasn't repaired.

The metal filler tube he shoved into his right pocket, the can of sealant he wedged into his left. Julian turned on the flashlight and clenched it between his teeth.

Slowly, and very carefully so not to get himself stuck, Julian manoeuvred around the fuel lines, bulkheads, and intakes. The heat of the working machinery caused sweat to pool on his brow. Every so often rivulets would corner his eyes and cause a saltine sting to force them closed. Moisture from the bilge heated, evaporated, and condensed on the engine. Every so often a drop would drip into Julian's open mouth. He gagged, but didn't drop the flashlight.

When he had finally positioned himself beneath the elbow in question, Julian pulled the metal filler from his pocket, unscrewed the cap, and squeezed the near-solid silver mixture into the crack. He held his palm over the spot while he fished the can of sealant from his other pocket. With a flick of his thumb he popped the cap off the can. He didn't even try to catch it, just let the lid fall into the muck below. If he couldn't get the leak fixed, it wouldn't matter anyway. Or so he rationalized.

After a few minutes of holding the filler in place, he removed his hand, and as he did, depressed the little white helmet of the sealant. A clear, varnish smelling spray coned out of the tiny hole and coated the intake elbow. Julian sprayed until there wasn't any sealant pressurized left to spray.

And then he counted.

Twenty-nine Mississippi's is when the first sprig of water pushed through the mixture and hung from the bottom of the elbow. It wasn't long after that the next drop escaped and joined the other. By the time Julian retreated to the gangway and was out from beneath the engine, the elbow was a steady drip.

He slammed the flashlight into the tub and bemoaned the situation. "How am I supposed to fix the leak if I don't have the right tools!"

Of course, nobody heard his frustration because he was in the engine room and both engines running meant nobody could hear anything in there, let alone Julian's own ears. If he could have, he may have been embarrassed over his outburst.

In the tool room, back at the shelves and digging through the milk crates, Julian wavered. He thought about ignoring the issue. If he was asked about the leak he'd simply assert that he'd fixed it. Then he thought about if the pipe burst while the ship slept, if he'd survive the mayday. But before he could think anything else, he fumbled across a wide black and red package. He pulled it from the crate and laughed at the emboldened 'As Seen on TV' logo at the top of the packaging. All the printed marketing promised success.

Instantly Stops Leaks! Super Strong Adhesive! Thick Rubberized Backing!

But it was the last one that caused Julian to suck his cheeks and wonder: Even Works Underwater!

"What the heck," he said, and prepared himself to head back under.

Julian dried the pipe with his rag and peeled the backing from the pre-cut section of black rubberized tape. He pressed it firmly over the crack and smoothed out all the little air bubbles.

And then he waited.

At one hundred Mississippi's he started to laugh.

In the tool room, he replaced the roll to the adhesives crate and shook his ahead. "Well," he said. "That was easy."

Chapter Nineteen: Embarkation

Julian tapped his fingers on the desk. He stomped his heel to the imaginary music in his head. It was finished. He wouldn't have to lie about fixing the leak when he hadn't. He wouldn't have to worry whether he'd survive the mayday if the pipe burst while the ship slept. They weren't going to sink. He rubbed his face, wiping his eyes last, then inspected the tiny clumps of sleep on each of his middle fingers. The knock on his door startled him. He quickly rubbed the little white boogers on his pants.

"Mind if I come in?" the female voice asked softly.

A quick scan of the room to make sure everything was neat and in order, and Julian opened the door to invite Tamara in.

"Everybody's all wound up about their battle today," she said in preface of her ask. "I don't think I'll—well, I really don't want to sleep back there tonight." She bit her thumb. She nodded to the empty bunk. "Can I sleep in Gilles bunk, just this once?"

Julian was out of his chair and making the bed before she'd finished. "Of course, yes," he stammered. "These are clean sheets—"

Tamara pulled his forearm. When he turned around her lips were on his.

The two engineers laid embraced upon the thin single mattress of Julian's top bunk. A wool fire blanket stretched across them, covering their naked bodies, but not long enough to cover their feet. Tamara's head rested in the crook of Julian's armpit. He breathed her hair. For some time, Tamara traced her fingers along the contours of Julian's bare chest, allowing her hand to rise and fall with the ship's gentle rock in the steady swell of the sea.

Outside the cabin door, at intervals of two-hours, a pair of feet shuffled down the hall. The wheel was turned on the fore cabin's hatch, opened, then delicately shut, but not sealed again. Words were exchanged in audible whispers, then the cabin door opened, closed, sealed, and the feet shuffled by Julian's cabin door once more.

Sentries were posted around the clock, shifts lasting two hours before fresh eyes were woken and stationed on the bridge. The clock-like arm of the radar blinked its circle round and around, undisturbed by even a single dot.

Julian and Tamara laid awake on the top bunk of single set of bunk beds in his engineer cabin. When he was certain the shift change had been completed and nobody was wandering the hall, he spoke.

"Do you want to get out of here with me?"

Tamara cooed. "Anywhere."

"No, for real," he said.

She looked at him. Her fingers quit tracing his nude body.

"Like, really, get out of here, leave the ship, rent a little cabin by the ocean and try us for a while?"

Tamara relaxed her head to his chest. Her fingers resumed their exploration, but she didn't speak.

"Things are getting out of control, Tam," he continued. "What are we even doing anymore?"

He flinched under the playful smack of her hand on his chest.

"You're thinking too much," she said. "It's an adventure as much as it is a cause. Do you know how many people would die to have your position? How many people email the organization every day begging for a spot on the crew? Any spot. Offering to pay even?"

"But warring with the locals?"

Tamara picked up Julian's limp hand and placed it on her head. She rubbed his hand to rub her hair, and when he picked up the effort, she settled again on his chest. "Just so you know, you're the worst pillow talker ever," she said.

"You've had a lot of Casanova's whispering in your ears, eh?"

That gentle caress of her delicate fingers stung like a scorpion when she pinched.

Julian yelped and swatted her grip from his nipple.

The two rolled in the tiny space, tickling and pinching, and like all playful tickling and pinching becomes, the two made love again, and slept until morning.

A firm knock on the door woke Julian from his dreamless sleep.

Ed entered the cabin and leaned against the bunk.

"We need the engines on," he said to Julian, then beckoned at Tamara, who pulled the blanket tight around her. "Good morning, Tamara." Ed smiled. "Captain's going to pull up the anchor and we're going to head back to San Felipe to pick up Jessie."

Tamara propped herself on elbows, holding the blanket over her chest.

"Jessie Treeville?" she asked.

Ed beamed. "The one and only."

"Sweet!" she said nearly dropping the blanket from around herself.

Julian sat up. "How soon does the captain want to get going?"

Ed hummed. "Like ten minutes ago."

"You got it," Julian said.

Ed began to close the cabin door when he peaked in a final time. "I better get an invite to the wedding."

A black Adidas sports bra hit him in the face. He stuck out his tongue, "Ooo—" he started to tease, but Julian snatched the underwear from him.

The breakwater wall of the harbour came into view as the crew's excitement peaked in its murmur of Jessie's arrival. A real OG. Jessie Treeville was one of the original six when Trident Legion used to risk everything, when Trident Legion held no punches, when Trident Legion kicked butt and didn't care who their adversary was, they were on a mission to conserve the oceans at all costs. Jessie Treeville was a god among legends.

One time, she dove beneath three patrol boats who'd netted a right whale and were pulling it toward the surface. She dove with a flashlight and a serrated blade, alone, under the three boats, under the rising net, and worked until she'd cut a hole large enough for the beautiful mammal to escape the certain death which stalked above. Sometime before it was safe to resurface her tanks ran out of oxygen. When Ed pulled her from the water she was unconscious and needed CPR to bring her back. After she spit up all the water the first words out of her mouth were, "That was easier than I thought, let's get on to the next one."

Jessie was Trident Legion, and in minutes she'd board the M/V Edward Abbey and kick the campaign into high gear.

A voice in broken English disrupted the fervour. "Something's burning and it's not in my kitchen," the stoic German said.

The cook rarely left his galley, and when he did, it was to sit alone on the fly deck, or read quietly in his bunk between meals. He didn't do shifts, he didn't pull in the nets, he didn't do chores. His only responsibility, as Julian rightfully noted in his argument with Tamara, was to cook. Which is a big enough responsibility with a crew of eighteen feeding three times a day.

He was good, better than good, and in his elite standards he maintained a tight kitchen of military cleanliness. His nose was sharp—despite looking like it'd been punched in once or twice in his lifetime—and on more than one occasion he'd picked up the scent of something askew long before there were eyes on the explanation and always long before anybody else noticed.

The turtle. The whale. Before Ed, before Tamara and Julian, before the captain or Tawd or Lisa or Ben or Rodriguez, both times the cook emerged from his galley and reported that something smelled rotten, and it wasn't his kitchen.

"Something's burning," he repeated. "And—"

"And it's not in your kitchen," Lisa chuckled.

He looked at her, visibly annoyed, shrugged, then lumbered back into the galley.

A grin clung to her face on the edge of an all out laugh.

Ed nudged her. "He's two-for-two, so far."

"I don't smell anything."

"I'll get the binos," Ed said. "Let's see what we can see."

The captain folded her mobile phone and set in on the chart table. She sucked her bottom lip. Ed noticed, but didn't say anything.

"What's Lisa have the crew doing?" she asked.

Ed held the binoculars at his side. "Well," he said. "The cook came up with another prophecy, said he smelled something burning, so we're going to have a peak and see what we can see."

The captain hummed.

Ed raised a hand like asking a question. His eyebrows scrunched.

"That makes him three-for-three," the captain said and forced a disappointed smile.

"Three-for-three? What burned?"

The Abbey purred into a near drifting speed. Ed set the binocular's back in their cradle.

"That was Jessie on the phone," the captain started. "Apparently, there's been an incident in town." She didn't look at Ed while she spoke. Her gaze remained over the breakwater wall and into the harbour. "Our little incident last night, well, in town they were staging the other half of the event."

The captain went on to relay what Jessie had reported. Her composure was that of a person who'd taken one too many dumb knockdowns, a biblical Job of real life, calm, bemused, in disbelief but not surprised. Ed slipped into his first mate's chair and listened in similar countenance. He learned of the public protest held outside the harbour gates. Of the hundreds of locals who showed up to the protest—not all of whom came in support of the cause, but by the end of the demonstration had all become united.

The captain shared how Jessie had been there too, observing from a distance, how at the end the orator took a can of black spray paint and sprayed the words Trident Legion on the hull of a white panga. When he'd added the skull and crossbones, someone threw a lit Molotov into the boat. The entire crowd cheered and hollered as the panga burned and the Trident Legion words melted away.

The captain put the Abbey into a complete drift, only several hundred metres from the harbour's entrance.

"Jessie said everybody began to disperse after the flames burned out. They'd said their piece, they'd destroyed something, take that Trident Legion. It's when the first of the pangas that attacked us came motoring in. Everything escalated from there. The panga teams told everyone that we attacked them as sea. Said how we threw lead and acid and tried to sink their fishing boats with our hoses."

"Jesus," Ed said. His eyes bugged. "Looks like we're not docking there tonight."

"They burned our dock."

"What?"

The captain chuckled. "Burned it. Like lit it on fire so that it is no more."

Ed rubbed his eyes. He palmed the lines on his forehead. "So, we're just going to grab Jessie and pull on out."

"She warned us to not even get close." The captain glanced at the radar then toward the harbour. "They probably already have people gearing up to come out here and take another swing. Jessie's down at the safe house. We're going to motor there, then send Ben and his panga team to get her."

"Then what? Where are we going to resupply? What about the rest of the campaign?"

"First we bring Jessie aboard," the captain said. "Then we wait to hear back from head office. I honestly don't know, Ed." She pulled the throttle and engaged the engines. The Abbey steered wide of the harbour and west up the coast. "You let the crew know about the change of plans— just not that we don't know what's happening next."

Chapter Twenty: Jessie

All except the captain and the cook were on deck when Ben slipped the panga against the Abbey's hull. Rodriguez clipped the painter line. Lisa leaned over the accommodation ladder and reached down to pull Jessie's bag aboard. Jessie slapped her hand away, slung the canvas knapsack over her shoulder, and scaled the ladder with one hand.

"What am I, first day at sea, I need you lifting my gear for me?" She glowered playfully at Lisa. "I'm just messing with ya, girl." She said and pulled Lisa in for a big bear hug. "Haven't seen you since, what, the Faroes?"

Lisa fixed her shirt. "I saw you in the Faroes, through my binos, as they herded you onto a navy RIB and stole you aboard the Iver Frigate." She shook her head.

"Oh, yeah," Jessie said, sincerely. "I forgot this time around ended that way."

"You're insane," Lisa said, eyes glowing in admiration.

Jessie laughed. "The one and only baby. You ready to have some fun?" She scrutinized each of the crew standing by. She nodded at Julian then asked Lisa, "Who's he?" and did this for each of the crew she didn't recognize. When her eyes met Rodriguez she guffawed and nobody was sure if it was in friendship or disgust. Jessie didn't offer any clarification.

"Is the German still cooking up grub?"

"Three times a day," Lisa said.

"Well, it's just about time for some eats, isn't it? My chops could use some filling."

With the knapsack slung over her shoulder, she looked like a caricature of the cool kid in high school, sunglasses dawned inside, pretending not to care attitude—only Jessie really did not care.

Just before she ducked into the companionway, she turned and put her hand on Lisa's shoulder. "Grab a plate, then you, Ed, and Ben meet me in the engineer's cabin."

Julian piped up, "My cabin?"

"You're hosting, Red."

"Red?" he asked.

Another guffaw. "Are you telling me all this time you've been on board, the only ginger, and nobody calls you Red?"

Julian blushed. Red was a pretty cool nickname.

The door was shut to prevent wandering ears from overhearing the conversation. Jessie brought Lisa, Ben, and Julian up to speed with the happenings in town. Ed confirmed everything she shared.

"None of this leaves the room," Ed added.

Jessie agreed.

"So, then what are you telling us for?" Ben asked.

Julian noticed a devious spark in his eyes but didn't know how to place it.

"When was the last time you refreshed yourself with the 'How to Sink a Ship' pam?" she asked, deadpan.

Ben clasped his hands. "Right. On."

For a minute the three veterans appeared lost in the memory of glory days. Julian wondered what his role in everything was, why Jessie had chosen him, if not only to commandeer his cabin, but assumed that if she wanted to use his cabin without his permission, she would have kept him on the other side of the door with the rest of the crew.

Upon closer inspection, Jessie's knapsack was more of a canvass army satchel than a knapsack. Olive drab and weathered leather straps wove through two metal gates securing the flap to the rest of the bag. She thumbed both latches, flipped the cover back, and ruffled through the contents. She smiled when she produced a small booklet, looked at it admiringly, then tossed it to land on Julian's lap.

"Learn the thing, Red," she said. "Then give it back."

He turned the booklet over and recognized the title immediately. "If this ever left the ship," Julian began droning. "If the public ever found out this was still our mandate, we'd lose all sorts of funding. Christ, don't even let it leave this room, not everybody on crew would be on board either."

Little gapes appeared between the lips of Lisa, Ben, and Ed. Jessie grinned ear to ear.

"I knew I liked you, Red." She snatched the booklet away and slipped it into her satchel. "Me and you are working point on this one."

Chapter Twenty-One: Counter-Attack

The light crept beneath the cabin door glowing its oppressive red. Julian couldn't sleep; he laid on his bunk, eyes open, Tamara nestled into his side snoring with abandon. The war that had him turned off the idea of campaign was now being brought home. And he'd have to participate.
He chortled.

Tamara shifted.

Julian grew up in a nominally Christian home. All that really meant was church on Sunday and youth group on Friday nights. Otherwise it was watching reruns of the Simpsons during the week and the occasional prayer before a test he hadn't studied for. Still, one tenant that never made sense to him was how people could rack up sins for things they didn't do. Sins of omission. The regular sins: pride, greed, wrath, envy, lust, gluttony, sloth, sure; but a guilty conviction for not doing something—that didn't seem fair. But staring into the red he realized that even though he hadn't thrown the acid, or sprayed the fire hose, or slingshotted lead at people, he was just as guilty as those who had, simply by being a part of the crew. A guilt he'd thus far been able to rationalize away. And now Jessie was calling him out, as if she spotted his apprehension, and wanted to take him to task. The action sin. The sin of commission. Guilt he could feel in his gut.

Julian thought he might pray, then his cabin door creaked open.

A ghostly figure highlighted in ephemeral red hovered beside his bunk.

"I hope you wrapped it up," the female voice scoffed. "Put your pecker in your pants and meet us on deck. We cast off in ten."

The door closed behind her. Tamara stirred.

"Who was that?" she asked.

"Captain wants the leak checked," he lied.

"Do you want me look?" Tamara asked.

He kissed her forehead. "No, no. You go back to sleep. It will only take a minute," he lied. Again.

Topside, Julian stepped from the ladder and into the panga were Ed and Lisa and Ben were already waiting.

"Tuck your tag or take it off," Jessie said coldly. "Do you want to get snagged up down there?"

"On my life jacket?" Julian wagered.

"Do you see any of us wearing one?"

He looked at each of them. No one wore theirs. Not one—Julian did a second take. "Is that grease on your face?" he asked.

"They have lights in the harbour, it will help keep our shine to a minimum," Lisa said.

Ed smudged his face enough to lather up his hand with the black grease. He wiped it on Julian's forehead before Jessie passed him the tube to apply it himself.

"Everybody ready?" Jessie asked. The first time she sounded somewhat concerned for the well-being of anybody other than the mission. "We might not all make it back, but—"

"What?" Julian interrupted.

"I'm just messing with you, Red," she said.

"But true," Ben said and patted him on the back. "Let's get out of here."

Julian unzipped his life jacket, slipped it off, and used it as a cushion instead.

They cast off from the Abbey. When they had paddled a good distance away, Ben fired up the engine and the team set course for the harbour to cut loose some pirate ships.

As they neared, Ben killed the panga's engine. It wasn't as if the Mexicans were night hawks, but some crew did sleep on the larger vessels, so the quieter the better. From seaside of the breakwater wall and all the way in, Ed and Lisa paddled discreetly.

The scent of doused timber and smouldering trash hung in the air. Where the Abbey's hundred-foot slip had moored only days before was now a puddle of nothing. The ladder from the landing, which rose and fell with the tide, descended to nothing. If they'd attacked us while we were docked and sleeping, Julian thought, and let the thought linger there.

Jessie whispered. "You two know what you're doing, right?"

Lisa and Ed nodded.

The panga scraped the bottom of the boat launch. Lisa stepped into the shallow water, then scurried up the ramp. Her shadow bounced along the road toward the main drag. She stopped where the fisherman had tied their pangas to the cleats. Ben picked up the paddles and steered the boat toward the string of pangas beneath the cleats where Lisa perched.

Seven boats, that's what Julian counted, seven pangas strung together and tied safely to the cleat above. The cleat Lisa crouched behind as she fiddled with the knot. When she had it loose, she laid the rope on the concrete, still looped around the cleat, but no longer tied, then climbed down the rebar ladder and into the first panga.

The docks creaked with idle concern as they always had in the dead of the night. The hulls of the steel trawlers, the ones not separated from each other by reclaimed rubber tires, scraped and clanged in gentle erosion as the ocean swell drifted in. The nearby gulls, floating on the surface, waiting the morning twilight when the fisherman would return to their ships and set out to sea for the day's catch, purred and cooed in anticipation.

A hand on Julian's knee startled him from his thoughts. "We're up," Jessie said.

They floated beneath the accommodation ladder of the last trawler in its three-ship sling.

"I don't feel good about this," Julian announced, albeit quietly.

"Yeah, well," Jessie said. "It's too late now, isn't it?" She didn't say what she said in malice, more how way leads onto way and where they've found themselves is at the bottom of an accommodation ladder hitched to a rusty Mexican trawler in the middle of the night, and well, it's a little bit late to be having second thoughts.

She gripped the first rung and started up the ladder.

Julian followed.

On the ship side of the gunwale they crouched to perform a listening halt. Julian opened his mouth to speak and Jessie snapped her index finger to his lips. She glowered at him as if to say, "Don't you dare."

If there were crew on the ship, there wouldn't be a polite exchange. There wouldn't be any way of explaining what two grease-faced Trident Legion insurgents were doing except for what it appeared that they were doing. Jessie reached into her satchel and pulled out an 18" pipe wrench. She handed it to Julian.

She whispered. "I'll do the one moored off, you do the middle, we'll meet back here and do the last before jumping ship."

The nod from Julian was hesitant, but a nod it was.

Jessie low shuffled across the deck to the opposing gunwale. When the two ships closed on each other she stepped into the next boat. She beckoned Julian with an arm overhead, and to his amazement, he sprung across the deck and climbed into the middle ship.

"You know where everything is," Jessie encouraged. "Just do your job." Even in the darkness, there was no mistaking her grin. Her face was lit by the moon. "Just forget the step where you shut off the water from filling the bilge." Jessie patted him on the back. "You good?"

It was the first time she'd shown concern for Julian specifically, and this display of humanity, somehow, was exactly the nudge he needed to step off the edge. He remembered the Faroes, all the stories of the Trident Legion raiding the whalers tool sheds and setting them ablaze. How the team risked physical harm to stop the slaughter of a thousand pilot whales, because, well, that's what they were there to do. Julian remembered his anger when Lisa called the mission and everybody retreated to their homelands with not having done anything. How he sat on the bluff, staring through the binos out to sea when the Iver Frigate had just commandeered the Abbey and with it, Jessie, reduced to her knees then escorted off the ship into the belly of the justice system.

And here she was, doing it all again. She believed. Jessie was Trident Legion.

A grin appeared on Julian's face as he remembered each reason he joined the organization to begin with. As he realized where he was and what he was about to do and who he was doing it with, his confidence peaked on the tips of his grin.

"I got this," he assured. And he believed.

Jessie continued her advance across the deck and onto the next ship.

Beneath the stern Lisa and Ed worked tirelessly with their own task. Whatever that was. Julian crept along the deck to the hatch nearest where he assumed would place him directly above the engine room.

Docked, engines off, he needn't worry about lifting the hatch and exploding the silence with the roar of metal machinery. Still, he slowly turned the latch and lifted the hatch just a crack to be sure.

When he was satisfied there wasn't any noise, or light, or anybody in the engine room, he opened it all the way and rested the hatch on its backstop. One last glance around the deck and he hopped down into the Mexican trawler.

Ed boarded their own panga from the stern. He tied the rope like a sports boat towing a skier—one end knotted through the port side eyelet and one end of the line tied to starboard eyelet. He joined both ends in the centre beyond the outboard motor. Using the moonlight to navigate, Ed flicked his wrists in routine precision, tied a figure-eight, and slipped a carabiner over the end. He reached for the lead line of the last panga. Holding the tow line's figure-eight in one hand, he flung his wrist around and finished a one-handed bowline, then depressed the gate on the carabiner and set the knot inside.

Lisa crouched in the first panga awaiting his signal.

With the string of pangas now secured to their own, Ed nodded to Ben, who grinned, then climbed into the little fishing boat. He stepped one to the other until he was crouched in the hull of the panga neighbour to Lisa. Overhead, the clatter of metal on metal, stole everyone's attention. Each held their breath waiting the fallout.

Jaw clenched furiously, Julian lay flat on the grated floor reaching for the pipe wrench leaning against the bulkhead in the bilge below. The words grinded from his snarled lips. "Stupid wrench." He reached harder for the dropped tool then decided to quit it. Julian never used a pipe wrench in his daily engineer tasks, he didn't need one for this either. It's basically the same drill as cleaning the valves. Make sure the wheel is secure in the off position. Spin the bar above the valve and remove the cover plate. As long as the valve is closed, he could leave the cover off all day and never worry about taking on water, however, turn the wheel on the valve and hundreds of gallons of water would blast through the pipe like a wrenched fire hydrant flooding into the street.

Hung over the lip of the grate, Julian placed his hands on the sea water intake valve for the ship's fire pumps. Above the valve, a foot away, the steel wheel waited.

He set the cover in the bilge, not that if he had left it lying on the grate if anybody attempted to stop the eruption of water they'd be able to secure it back over the valve—they wouldn't—only to keep it from falling as his wrench had and risking again being discovered by his clamouring clumsiness.

Better do both, he thought, and shuffled to the opposite side of the room. He repeated the steps, this time without dropping anything. He exhaled heavily. The path to the ladder was free of obstruction. His heart crept up his throat and began marching. Julian's hands trembled as he set them on the valve wheel.

He inhaled, cracked the seal, then spun the wheel as fast as he could. Water burst through the open housing and waterfalled off the ceiling. A steady crush of pressurized water echoed relentlessly. He ran to the first valve, set his hands, spun the wheel, and jumped back as the water erupted on the starboard side of the ship. He flashed across the room and was three rungs up the ladder when he looked over his shoulder. Two steady sprays, like renegade fountains, showered the sleeping engine room. Already, the water had filled the bilge and was splashing at the grated walk way. His heart raced.

On deck he wagged his head wildly, certain a gang of Mexican fisherman were advancing with crowbars and chains to beat him into the other side of living. And then he heard it. Two clicks of a tongue in cheek, a pause, then twice more from the trawler he'd first climbed into.

Jessie cocked her head and whispered sharply, "Let's go."

Julian looked around. There were no Mexicans, no gang, just an empty harbour, like when he'd gone below, only now, the ship moored to the pier was sinking beside his own trawler, which was quickly sinking beside the trawler where Jessie waited. Otherwise, things were surprisingly quiet. Calm even.

He ran to the hull wall and reached toward Jessie. She ran to the edge and grabbed one of his hands. "You have to jump, Red." But he was already airborne.

His feet pressed off the lip as Jessie pulled and somehow, barely, he managed to swing a foot over the side of the last sinking trawler's gunwale. A shift of his weight and a quick shimmy and he was sprawled on the deck of this last boat.

Jessie grabbed his hand and raised him up, before hustling to where they first boarded, then slid down the accommodation ladder into the belly of the waiting panga. Julian was only a step behind when Ben fired up the engine. Safely landed, Ben put the throttle into mid-gear.

It was slow moving, towing seven pangas behind, but pangas are persistent little boats with determined little engines and once the littlest bit of traction was found it was a steady climb out of the harbour.

Lisa pulled the line from the cleat then reached into the transom.

A hiss of water sprayed. She held the little plug between two fingers, inspecting it in the moonlight, kissed it, then hopped into the next boat. Water had already begun filling. She passed Ed and stumbled into the fourth panga in the series. When all the transom plugs were pulled and both Ed and Lisa were safe inside their own panga, the engine quit.

"Are you kidding me!" Julian snapped, terrified they'd just lost all hope of escape.

A steady dinosaur moan reverberated from inside the harbour. Flashlights bounced along the malecón toward the groaning noises. The unmistakable tightening of braided docking lines, the staccato creak before too much tension snapped the thickness, hurried its warning across the water.

"Slip the beaner." Ben said.

Ed reached over the stern and cut the carabiner free from the water-logged tow.

One by one, beginning with the furthest away, each of the seven pangas slipped beneath the surface and disappeared without even a gurgle.

Julian realized the engine hadn't died, and in realizing, started to laugh.

The anxious snap shot through the air like an unseen bullet. The ships were going under.

This time, Ben threw the throttle into high gear and the five of them bounced along surface toward the mother ship.

Chapter Twenty-Two: Celebration

The cabin was smaller than Julian remembered. He'd only ever been it it once before, and that on strict engineer business, but it seemed smaller than he remembered. A pile of Trident Legion swag clogged the unused sink. The kitty-corner bathroom—the head—was awkwardly positioned adjacent the cabin door and was encroached upon by the abnormally large cedar computer desk. A silver industrial laptop, keys weathered from years of use by transient crew, rested on the desktop. "Get 'er done," bounced around the black screen in a twisting three-dimensional algorithm.

Ed opened the cupboard above the dormitory-sized refrigerator. He removed a glass bottle of crystal liquid. The glass was embossed with silver lettering.

"Blue Agave," Lisa said approvingly.

"Blue Agave," Jessie repeated. She lined up five plastic cups on the computer desk.

Ed poured generously, capped the bottle, and returned it to the cupboard.

When everybody had their cup in hand and were ready to cheers, Julian interrupted.

"Blue Agave?" he said. "What am I missing?"

Ben grinned.

"Tradition," Ed offered.

"You are green, aren't you?" Jessie mocked. "Maybe I should change your name.

Julian couldn't help but blush.

"There it is," she laughed, nudging his shoulder like old friends.

Ed rested his arm around his shoulder. "At the beginning of every campaign," Ed began, "The first mate buys a bottle of tequila, each country has its own brand: The Faroes is Patron, Panama is Ueta, Mexico is Blue Agave. Captain turns a blind eye as long as it stays in my cabin and only comes out after a successful operation."

"You mean the captain knew about tonight?" Julian asked.

Lisa shook her head. "Not exactly."

Ed straightened up. He turned the plastic cup of tequila around in his hand. "If we would have been caught," he said, letting the thought hang. "If something would have happened, one of us got hurt, went down with a ship, the captain needs plausible deniability."

The lines on Julian's brow furrowed.

"Trident Legion needs plausible deniability," Jessie corrected.

"If something happened, it needed to be because we acted alone, rogue of Trident Legions mandate."

"We would have been hung out to dry," Julian muttered.

"That's why the tradition," Ed said, raising his glass. "We get things done because we ride on the shoulders of giants—all the people who have gone before us."

Smiles stole the corners of each crew member's face. They raised their glasses, and to Julian's surprise, his arm raised too, and he realized he was grinning along with the rest.

"Down the hatch," the collective voice spoke. Each gulped the shot.

The aesthetic sting of hard tequila burned the back of Julian's throat before he swallowed. The liquor warmed his chest and coated his stomach in pungent discomfort. He swallowed the saliva forming in his mouth. Ben suggested another round to which everybody agreed. Except Julian. He excused himself, and to his relief, nobody chastised him. Instead, as he was about the close the cabin door behind him, Jessie spoke and her words were sincere.

"You're one of us now, Julian," she said. "You are Trident Legion."

He looked at Ed. "Now I get why you wouldn't let me say 'Down the hatch,' before."

Ed winked. And like all winks it admitted one in on the gaff. They were equals now.

If Julian was planning to sleep, he wouldn't get it. Tamara was lying in his bunk, eyes eerily open under the red-light glow. He didn't notice this until he was nearly on top of her.

"I thought you were checking the leak," she said flatly, voice accusatory as they come.

Julian slid under the covers. He lay on his back. Tamara didn't cuddle up to him like she'd become accustom to doing.

"They tapped you, didn't they?"

"I'm tired, Tamara. I just want to sleep."

She sniffed the air. When she sat up, she pulled the covers with her.

"You smell like tequila."

Julian covered his face. He rubbed his eyes and yawned.

"Ow!" he yelped. His hand quick to grip the spot where she punched.

"You went on a mission and got the shot!"

He wasn't sure if she was jealous or excited or both. The only thought going through his mind was how was he the only one who didn't know what went on while the rest of the ship slept? More, how had he forgotten all the rumours of such things?

In the Faroes he'd heard all the stories, wanted to be part of the stories, part of the action, and sulked when he couldn't be. Now, here, in Mexico, he'd helped scuttle ships. No, he'd scuttled a ship himself, and he wasn't quite sure how he felt about it. That thing about wanting something, getting it, and then the thing not being what was wanted after all. That's what was going through his mind. The tequila didn't help.

"I'm so jealous," Tamara said. She settled down beside him. "You have to tell me everything." Her fingers traced his shoulders and chest.

"In the morning," Julian said. "I'm beat."

Tamara wiggled her way down the single mattress. Her hands reached for Julian's pants.

"I know what will help you sleep," she whispered.

Before Julian could object, she had him in her grip.

Water slapped the Abbey's hull in rolling rhythmic riding. The bow raised and lowered as the ship cut through the water toward La Paz. In under an hour, the Abbey would be passing the Vaquita refuge for the last time on their way out of the Sea of Cortez and into the international waters of the mighty Pacific Ocean on route to San Diego, in the great United States of America. A tactical retreat. The campaign had been called on account of safety concerns. Still, nobody seemed to mind.

Rumours of the previous night's activities had penetrated the cabin bulkheads where now everybody was giddy with nostalgia. Rodriguez found some old Trident Legion films, self-produced by the crew of earlier campaigns who suffered long passages across arctic waters in the inaugural days of the organization. The crew had scripted horror flicks where contaminated beans, dented in their cans, had poisoned everybody on board except the engineers who were busy in the engine room doing engineer things during breakfast. When the grease covered grunts emerged from the engine room to finally dig in to some chow, everybody was passed out on the benches, foaming at the lips—some convulsing even.

The story went that when the engineers tried to resuscitate the bosun and first mate, the bosun and first mate roared to life and sunk their newly sharpened and thirsty teeth into their throats. Only one engineer managed to escape and the rest of the film was him hiding in various compartments on the ship, desperately trying to reach the bridge where he could radio for help. The movie cuts to credits when he's finally reached the bridge and has his hand nearly on the radio receiver, the door bursts open with the other two engineers foaming at the lips, mouths wide full of sharpened teeth, and diving toward the lone survivor.

There were others. Comedies making a mockery of whale hunters, dull harpoons and three-stooge like slapstick choreography tripping on uncoiled rope, casting hooks and catching the waistband of another crew, sending them overboard. Four movies in total. Another tradition, Julian learned, after a successful mission against the campaign's adversary. Even though none of the others had been tapped, the success promised that there would be future opportunities. The success of the mission meant Trident Legion was still relevant.

The perpetrators got hard liquor; the rest of the crew got vintage films.

By the end of the day, the Abbey would be rounding Cabo and home free. Well, nine days home free, but at least they'd be in open waters and out of the vengeful reach of the Mexican poachers and trawlers and protesters alike. They'd be safe after what proved to be somewhat of a troublesome campaign.

The only disappointment, shared by all and spoken by none, was that nobody had glimpsed a Vaquita marina dolphin. At least it was sobering to know there hadn't been any drowned in the nets they'd retrieved, and none of their carcasses had been washed up on shore like so many common bottle-nose dolphins had during their tenure in San Felipe.

At least there was that.

Chapter Twenty-Three: Vaquita

Julian and Tamara monitored the engine room closely. Both engines appeared to be running smoothly with the adhoc 'As Seen on TV' patched intake. As long as the captain didn't jump the throttle, and as long as the weather held out on their journey home—and all reports indicated smooth sailing—the engineers were confident the seal would hold. Once in dry dock, the issue could be properly addressed.

Tamara was as giddy as the rest of the crew and googled over Julian whenever he passed. Eventually they found themselves alone in the tool room. Julian knew she wouldn't stop until he told her. It wasn't like Jessie and them said that he couldn't, only he figured it was one of those things he wasn't supposed to talk about. The first rule of Fight Club is you don't talk about Fight Club.

"I already know what y'all did," she whined. "You might as well tell me your part."

She turned over a homer bucket and sat down.

Julian hummed, pretending to mull over her prodding.

Tamara rolled her eyes. "Stop being so coy. You know you want to tell me. It's only the dream of everybody on crew."

"You start," Julian said. If she already knew everything and he only clarified some of the details for her, he really couldn't get in trouble with Jessie and the rest. At least that's what he reckoned.

With remarkable detail, Tamara described the evening previous, from when Julian left the bed, to when he returned, and only missed the detail where he'd dropped the pipe wrench in the bilge of the trawler.

He didn't correct her.

"So, is it true?" she asked.

"That's pretty bang-on," Julian said, honestly aghast. "Does everybody know that?"

She smirked. "Only in hushed tones and grins. Unofficially, of course."

The radio interrupted. "Engineer, engineer, engineer."

Julian answered the call and the captain informed him that she would be killing the starboard engine and dropping the throttle into drift while keeping the port side engine idling at ready.

He slipped the radio into his cargo shorts' pocket. "That's weird," he said, stroking his non-existent beard.

"It's a straight shot to La Paz then out. I don't know why we'd pause and give anyone a chance at retaliation?" Tamara said.

Julian scrunched his face. "Retaliation for what?" He stared at Tamara. "Nothing happened last night."

Tamara returned his stare with an unsure look of her own.

Julian winked. "I'm going up to see what's going on."

Tamara moaned a short sexually provocative groan as he exited the room. For the first time since boarding the panga the night previous, Julian thought maybe, just maybe, he could get used to all the attention.

Ed, Lisa, Jessie, and the captain were all on the bridge when Julian entered. There were no exchanges of self-gratification. There were no giddy blinders over anyone's eyes. The mood was solemn. The usually livening saltine air was heavy and grave. Julian whitened. Something was very wrong. He felt like throwing up.

"What's," he started. Whatever was simmering in his stomach reached the back of his throat and he swallowed hard to keep from ralphing.

Ed stared at the floor; his head swayed slightly as if he were shaking it in disbelief. "We picked something up on the radar," he said. "Just outside the refuge."

Julian steadied himself on the chart table.

"PROFEPA is out there now, them and a navy RIB." Ed paused as if to weigh his words. After tonguing several and uttering none, he finally said, "They claim to have four floaters."

The bridge blurred as if they were sailing through a morning fog. Julian's legs softened. He tried to speak but everything went black.

Somebody was slapping his cheek. A woman's voice spoke. Like when the bridge began to blur, his vision slowly reversed. Julian did not know where he was. The ceiling was covered in wires and tubes. The occasional metallic box was dotted with LED lights and rectangular LED screens. A mouthpiece attached by a long-spiralled cord rested neatly in its cradle. The air smelled like ocean, moreover, it smelt like rotting flesh preserved in salt. It smelled like the day they found the whale, or the turtle, or—it smelt like when he was a kid, at the beginning of summer, him and his dad de-winterizing the fishing boat and opening the live well to rinse it out and having the contained rot of a forgotten fish dart up his nostrils and down his throat. He gagged.

"There you are, tough guy," the voice said. It was Lisa.

Julian looked around. Jessie and Ed were huddled, the captain didn't acknowledge. Lisa stared down at him, her face a foot from his, when he realized he was laying in her lap.

"You're the one keeping the engines running, huh?" Jessie mocked.

Lisa tried not to giggle, but it was no use. "You fainted," she chuckled. "I don't think I've ever said those two words ever in my entire life."

He exhaled as he propped himself on his elbows. "I—I don't know—" and then he remembered. "Four floaters, like people?"

Confusion stole the room. Even the captain glanced over her shoulder. Ed titled his head and tugged his ear.

"What? No," he said. A flutter of realization graced his face. "Makes sense why you did the old fish flop, I guess."

Julian used the chart table to pull himself to standing. Through the glass he saw the grey navy RIB drifting near the orange PROFEPA boat. Both vessels looked to be leaking something. A thick rainbow film floated on the surface of the sea and transmuted like a kaleidoscope, shapes of purple and green and pink and blue. If not for the ominous hackles on Julian's neck, he would have commented that the sea looked like a painting.

He gripped the ledge of the chart table. His jaw limped ajar as his free hand raised reflexively to cover his mouth. Four black shadows dotted the oil covered water. Julian's head shook rapidly like his mind re-fused to accept what was coming through his eyes. He bit his knuckle.

"Are those—" but he couldn't say the word.

Jessie finished his question. "Vaquita." Her eyes never wavered from the four floating carcasses.

Chapter Twenty-Four: Exile

The Abbey approached the two smaller vessels, but before the captain could bring the ship alongside, the navy RIB fired up its engines and intercepted the cutter's advance. Two uniformed crew members, ultramarine from cap to boot, snapped their arms chest to outstretched finger tips, in the direction of La Paz. Their faces seethed.

"Are they telling us to leave?" Lisa wondered out loud.

The UHF radio crackled with Spanish admonitions.

"Not welcome?" Lisa attempted a translation.

The captain steered around the navy vessel. The four shadows, the lumps floating on the sea, became clearer as they approached. Their light grey skin was light grey no more. They were smooth with shine, but not only shine, there were patches of brown and what almost looked like the edges of paper where fire started to burn, like something small had been eating outward-in on their skin. One of the Vaquita had deep welts, similar to the burn marks on the others, only these were pits of pulpy, blackened flesh.

They appeared to have been dead a long time.

If not for the oil on the water, if these Vaquita were come across during a regular patrol, one might easily get the impression that these dolphins were caught by fisherman and dumped to avoid repercussion. But afloat inside this spill, the thought never crossed any minds.

"We have to do something," Lisa said.

"What can we do?" Jessie barked. Not maliciously; cold.

She was right. The Vaquita were already dead. Like all the Vaquita before. And all the Vaquita that were left. On a long enough timeline extinction is natural.

The captain narrowed her eyes at the uniformed navy crew members as she steered the ship away from the spectacle. Without looking at Lisa, she said, "Have your crew secure everything on deck. Anything we can stow, stow it. Once we make the turn around Cabo, it's going to get rough and I want everybody inside."

The frayed black and white flag grumbled on its mast punctured by the wind in a snapping march. The angry skull and crossbones glared at the sea, over the waters, and into the white clouded sky.

The fore deck was vacant of all the lead, floats and buckets. There were no clothes tied to the stanchions to dry. No towels. The folding chairs had been stowed. It almost looked orderly. Respectable even. Except for the flag. The flag was mean. Intimidating. Even if one of the bones was a shepherd's staff and not the traditionally threatening sword.

Over head the sky was blue, dotted only with the occasional pencil-like cloud. It's over the bow where the sky turned white. Foreboding.

Below deck, Rodriguez re-wrapped the cords he'd scavenged to connect the laptop to the TV in order to celebrate the earlier victory with those homemade videos. The TV was secured behind the whiteboard. The mugs and dishes were locked under the counter. All around the ship sullen crew stowed breakables, secured belongings, returned items to their homes where while on campaign it was permittable to leave things lying around, but entering open waters where the little 110-foot cutter would be battered by the disinterested ocean, anything not secure could become a projectile intent on injuring a crew member, or worse, damaging the ship and putting all their lives at risk.

Although none of the other crew had seen the dead Vaquita, like the secrecy of the prior evening's mission, everybody knew. Only this time, nobody dared utter a word. Maybe if it wasn't spoken of, the pain of failing the only task they'd ventured into Mexico for, didn't have to be true. Denial is quite the drug.

When everything was secured, or mostly everything, one-by-one, people returned to their bunk and slipped on headphones, or pulled their curtains closed, or slipped on sleep masks to shut out the world. Everybody did everything they could to manufacture the illusion of privacy, as it was impossible to truly be alone onboard the Abbey. Everybody always knew everything.

Tamara refused to speak to Julian as both of them worked to secure the engine room. Her googling had been replaced with disdain. Whenever she passed, if she even gave a look—which most times she deliberately avoided doing—her eyes were cold, flat; all of her features pallor; she avoided even brushing him. Once, Julian is certain, she even spit as he skirted by with the coiled bilge tubes. He was sure of it, but didn't want to believe; not Tamara.

Julian removed his ear defenders. He hung his safety glasses on the hook above the tool chest. Tamara, with her back to him, did the same, then started out of the room.

"Tamara," Julian said.

She opened the tool room door.

Julian grabbed her elbow. "Please, Tamara," he begged.

Her recoil was visceral. She snapped: "Don't touch me!" Then slammed the door.

Julian collapsed to the upturned homer bucket and twisted his knuckles into his eyes. He wiped away whatever sleep had accumulated in the corners and rested his head in his palms.

A drumbeat, his heart, thumped in his temples.

He closed his eyes and thought about all the things which brought him on board the Abbey to begin with, then tumbled down a regret filled hole.

It was so easy in the beginning. It all made sense. Once he learned that he was born into privilege, middle-class, and white, it was a no-brainer. He had to do something. What did the church teach? Repentance, penance, and paying for your sins. Is that how he got here? First the YouTube clips about those poor little chickens hurried down the conveyor belt, chicks just hatched and furry instead of feathers, the kind you want to pick up and kiss and rub against your face, rushing down the conveyor belt and through the grinder, screaming. One brave faceless worker had dared to break the gag order and filmed the ten-second piece and released it online exposing the atrocity to the world. Then it was the factory farms and the meat conspiracies and Food Inc.—almost too horrible to watch. Admittedly not enough to turn him vegan, but definitely turned on to the vegetarian side of good and evil. How could he not? There was nothing he could do to change the privilege he was born into, but he could make reparations by using his privilege to do some good. Those videos led to Greenpeace videos led to murmurs of the Animal Liberation Front, and before he knew it he was glued to the Trident Legion feed cheering on Jessie and the crew as they did their part to actively combat the outfits colonizing the oceans and raping its bounty. All gung-ho and fired-up he filled out the online application and signed himself up for the first available position: a pay-your-way spot onto the crew campaigning in the Faroe Islands. The grindadrap. GrindStop. Getting between the barbaric slaughter and the whales. Saving lives. Doing something actually, not just 'liking' and sharing a post. The real deal. And then—

"You should just kill yourself," the man's voice said sternly.

Julian looked up from where he sulked.

Tawd towered in the entrance.

"Excuse me," Julian said, teeth grinding. Where the aggression came from, he did not know.

"I wouldn't go wandering around the deck alone if I were you. Open waters, rough seas, if you fell in, someone might not notice until morning. Awfully hard to find a scrawny little dip like you in such a big bowl of ocean."

Julian stood. Anger from the base of his spine surged up his back and into his eyes. Each finger closed tight into a fist; their fingernails dug into his palms so tightly that if he squeezed any harder there would have been blood. Unconsciously, his eyes scanned the room and settled on the pipe wrench hung in its place on the wall. He looked deep into Tawd's eyes. "Are you threatening me?"

Tawd was not intimidated, in fact, Tawd grinned. "A lot of people are going to feel the same way when I tell them what you did."

"I think you should go," Julian said, sharpening his tone.

Tawd leaned over Julian, forcing him to look up.

"You poured that oil overboard."

If eyes could die, Julian's did. His surge of confidence waned. His face softened. Two fingers tapped Julian's chest with such force he thought he'd bruise.

"You killed those Vaquita," Tawd said, and poked him again. "You better watch your step."

The adrenaline wore off and Julian found himself alone in his cabin. It wasn't true, he kept telling himself. Those Vaquita were already dead. It wasn't possible. Not that fast. Not at all even. The way their bodies were peppered with rot. Something got to them first.

He set his radio in the charger, turned the volume knob to ten, and climbed into his bunk. "It's not my fault," he whispered. And slipped into a dream plagued sleep.

Chapter Twenty-Five: Incubus

It was summertime, Boston. The sun blazed in the blue midday sky. The water lapped lazily at Julian's feet where he stood at the water's edge. Slowly, he walked forward into the chilling expanse. When he was far enough out, deep enough to cover his waist, he dove headlong into the swells. After swimming for some time, he reclined into the ocean and floated on its surface, ears submerged, listening, as the sun dried the salt exposed on his skin. He listened to his heart beating in his chest. He listened to the pilgrim bubbles rising sporadically to the surface. If he listened hard enough, he could hear the fleeting garbled tones of whales from somewhere in the deep.

And then it happened.

The screech of metallic abrasion pierced the tranquil waters. The sporadic bubbles multiplied into a nebula of suspended molecules vibrating in violent succession. The screeching, the chalkboard nail-dragging assault, which had signalled this eco-ambush, was overtook by the rumbling roar of a solvent stampede.

The ocean quaked.

Julian bolted upright and treading, arms like knives spreading butter, legs peddling to remain afloat—but it was no use. A waterfall of astringent green poured over him, blotting out the sun. The eruption filled his eyes and ears and nose and throat with fetid grime, choking him, each breath drawing more of the liquid inside his lungs.

When he could no longer endure the pummelling, when he was certain he would surely drown, in a stroke of compassion gifted from King Triton himself, Julian floated to the surface and away from the runoff's fallout.

The sewage poured into the ocean, layered surface to deep, and expanded like a conical ripple as far as he could see. Fish from 20,000 leagues descended upon and feasted on the stool waste as greedy fisher-man cast their nets over the bounty and set their catch on the plates of un-aware peoples enjoying a Friday night fish fry.

Julian startled awake, sweat soaked though his t-shirt. A hand reached across his body. He sprung up, smashed his head against the water pipe, but still managed to scoot back on the mattress, fists up to defend himself.

"Jeeze," Tamara said with a hint of berating. "Overreact much?"

A sighed escaped Julian's mouth as his tensed body relaxed. "I thought you were—"

"I don't care. I'm only here to get my sweater."

She tugged at the black hoodie tangled in the sheets of the bed.

"Tamara," Julian started.

She yanked the sweater free and turned to leave.

"Tamara, please," he whined. "What's going on? What did I do to make you so upset? One minute your gushing and now this?"

The smack of her open palm on the cabin door had him flinch.

"What's going on?" she sassed. "What did you do?" She stepped to-ward him. "Are you kidding me? Are you stupid?"

Julian flushed. He noticed himself biting his lower lip and released it.

She continued her advance. "Have you forgot those dozen buckets of sludge we put overboard—no—correction—that you dumped overboard. And just outside the refuge! Those poor animals never stood a chance. You murdered them! What did I do? Give me a break."

Julian sat aghast.

"You wanted the campaign to end. You've wanted to go home since the moment you got here."

Julian sneered. "You know that's not true."

Tamara jerked her head away. She gagged. "I can't even look at you without feeling nauseous. You make me sick."

Something caught Julian's attention. He titled his head just noticeably. His eyes narrowed on her outstretched finger. In the midst of the argu-ment, after being jarred from a restless sleep, Tamara yelling at him, finger pointing, in this very moment he noticed a slight crook to what should have been a straight finger.

"What are you looking at?" Tamara snapped.

"Has your finger always been crooked?"

She made a fist. Her ears poured smoke.

Before she slammed the door behind her, she flared her nostrils. "And I was never gushing. You were just the closest thing at the time."

A chortle escaped his nose. He fell back on his pillow with a sigh. "Has everybody on this ship gone mad?"

Chapter Twenty-Six: Sickness

After a short refuel in La Paz the M/V Edward Abbey was positioned to make the turn around Cabo. Even before the ship passed the last protective stretch of land, everybody could feel where they were. If the Sea of Cortez was a kiddy pool in a neighbour's backyard, the Pacific was a waiver-required wave pool just outside the big city. The refurbished Coast Guard Cutter rocked at angles so threatening that if anybody had been on deck they would have surely gone over.

An unsecured tablet on the chart table crashed to the floor. Shards of glass detonated from its screen. The Abbey rocked again. The shattered tablet slid with the roll and bounced down the stairs into the media room.

Unaccustomed to the violent swell, whoever wasn't seated or lying down, were thrown into each other, or into the bulkheads, or against the bolted down tables in the mess. Colour drained from faces as quickly as if accosted by a ghost, only the skin didn't turn white, they became shades of yellow and lupus green.

Only a few people appeared unperturbed by the new circumstance aboard the Abbey. If the captain felt the heaviness of the sea, she maintained her composure like a captain who had spent years on the water—who was born to the ocean. She didn't seem affected at all.

Rodriguez wasn't bothered either. In fact, while everybody else was lined up outside the heads waiting to spew, or breathing into paper bags to keep from spewing, or lying in their bunks with cold wash cloths spread over their foreheads, eyes closed, choking down breaths; he sat in the mess eating a box of Oreo cookies. And he looked happy.

"Where'd you get those from?" Julian asked when he entered the mess.

Rodriguez swallowed the cookie in his mouth. With thumb and index finger he pinched the next Oreo in line, inspected it, then shoved the entire cookie down his trap. He chomped as he spoke. "My whole duffel bag is Oreo's."

"What?"

He chomped some more. Little black crumbs escaped his mouth and landed on the table. Rodriguez pressed his finger over each crumb until he had a small black lump on the tip of his pointer. He set his finger to his lips, sucked it clean, then wiped the finger dry on his pant leg.

"So, I like Oreo's. That's not a crime. They're vegan. I can bring as many as I want."

Julian opened the cupboard below the counter. Three mugs crashed haphazardly to the floor and shattered. "Rats," he said.

"Meh," said Rodriguez. "That's nothing. I'm pretty sure I heard someone's laptop smash upstairs."

"Upstairs? Like the bridge."

"You know what I mean."

"People don't fair so well in the rougher waters, eh?"

"Doesn't bother me."

"Yeah, I guess me neither." Julian chucked his chin toward the tray of Oreo's. "Mind if I have one?"

Rodriguez faked a smile only a Mexican could fake. "I only brought enough for me."

The Pacific rolled the Abbey for three days straight. The crew's daily routine had been abandoned, as nobody was allowed on deck. A safety brief was given by the captain—more a directive—if anybody ventured outside, the captain would personally throw the son-of-a-gun overboard. Despite not being sick or appearing fatigued, the captain's short tone definitely meant the rough waters were getting to her. The captain was generally stoic leader and bright eyed and bushy tailed Pollyanna camera girl. But not now. Not in open waters.

Instead of cleaning the deck, or sorting nets, or painting this, or mending that, the crew remained in their cabins. Some, having become accustomed to the steady roll, watched videos on their laptops. Others attempted a game of cards in the mess. This, however, did not last long.

Every card played ended up sliding off the table and fluttering to the floor. Even if they managed to keep the cards on the table, the brain power required was much more than what was available and quickly ushered the card players to the nauseated side of camp. Most, however, remained in their bunks fighting the urge to vomit, or if unable to, were doubled over one of the only two toilets below deck, taking turns spewing into the metal bowls.

The desperate convulsion of a reflux scraping bowels for a teaspoon of bile to vomit lurched from inside the head near Julian's cabin. The person inside, unable to mutter a word, completely slave to his body's pummelling, sounded minutes from death. Julian listened with horrific concern. It was Tawd.

At first, Julian was filled with condescending delight when he'd seen Tawd scamper through the mess and into the hallway outside the engineer cabin. His swaying side to side. His covering his mouth with one hand while holding his stomach with the other, thighs tight as if he were clenching a golf ball between his butt cheeks, was a sight acutely satisfying. When the tides change from oppressee to oppressor there is no gradient scale of virtue. It's vengeance. Tawd, destroyed by the sea, became extremely pleasurable to Julian, a serves-you-right kind of satisfaction. But that was forty-minutes past, and now, listening in horrific awe, his self-righteous gloating had withered into daunting concern.

The guy sounded like he would die.

Anybody moving from the fore cabin to the mess, on hearing one of Tawd convulsions, shivered in terror, looked in at Julian and asked without speaking, eyes saucers, hands in question, Is Tawd going to be okay? Julian would suck his lips and nod, though not quite believing himself.

Finally though, Julian acted.

Beneath his desk, Velcroed to the side of his mini-fridge was an emergency first-aid kit. A small red rectangular bag with a white cross and a little tab that read St. John's Ambulance. Julian peeled it from the fridge and unzipped the flap.

He thumbed through the various gauze, tapes, and bandages to find the single use packets of anti-seasickness pills. The kit had everything even sewing gear. He pulled out the pills and made a mental note to keep the first aid kit when he left the ship. A souvenir which might come in handy one day.

He knocked on the door but only a moan responded.

"It's Julian, Tawd."

Tawd muffled a gag. "Go away, I'm fine."

A scratching haul of sea-otter bark echoed around the small room and through the door. Julian quivered.

"You're not fine, I'm coming in." He tried the handle, but it was locked. "Open the door, Tawd," Julian said, jaw clenched.

A moment later, the lock clicked over. Julian turned the knob and pushed the door open. Tawd laid on the ground, feet outstretched toward the stainless-steel shower, torso hunched over the toilet bowl, hands gripping the rims, his long, unkempt dreads hung all around and inside the soiled metal goblet.

Julian shook off the grin which sprung to his cheeks at the sight of a defeated Tawd. "Come on," he said. "Sit up. You need to take this." He held a bottle of water in one hand and the small tablets pinched between his fingers in the other. "It's a little bit late, but two should give you some relief. Come on. Or you can die here on the floor."

Tawd lifted his head and glanced over his shoulder. His eyes were clouded. Drool hung from his pierced lip. He swallowed. "I'm not your friend," he said, and dropped his face into the bowl. It was as if uttering those words expended all the energy he had left in his body.

Julian slapped the pills on the counter. He dropped the water bottle into the sink.

Julian straddled Tawd's legs. "A jerk to the bitter end, eh? Well, not on my watch." He bent down in a squat, tugged at Tawd's closest arm and slung it around his neck. He slipped his other arm around Tawd's shoulder and under his armpit. He stood, at least he tried to stand, but it was no use.

"Alright big guy, you're going to have to help me." He tugged again. "Up. Up. Up." He commanded like a drill sergeant. "Let's go."

Slowly and strenuously, Tawd helped right himself to standing. Julian timed the roll of the ship to shuffle Tawd from the head, down the hall and into the engineer cabin. One last roll and Julian flopped Tawd onto the bottom bunk.

He returned with the pills and the water bottle. "Now sit up and swallow these. I know you might not want to and we're not friends and whatever else, if not for your own saving, do it for the Legion. You're useless in this shape." He held out the anti-sickness medication again. "Take the pills, rest, and get your legs back. You can't tough guy through this. Be smart."

Tawd groaned. Eventually, he sat up. He accepted the pills and water and swallowed them one at a time.

"I'm going to bring you a cold clothe, just lay down, see if you can't close your eyes for a bit."

The radio, silent in its cradle beside the bunk, shook as it blasted three calls for engineer.

Tawd trembled at the sudden alarm.

Julian snatched the radio and turned down the volume. Then he apologized to Tawd. "Sorry," he said. "I had it turned up so it would wake me if I fell asleep."

Tawd closed his eyes and shook his head disapprovingly.

After a sigh, Julian held the radio to his lips and answered the call.

"It's your shift," Tamara said, her insolence iceberg cold. "Engineer, out."

"Out?" Julian said, not into the receiver, but to himself. "Did she just out me?"

He looked at Tawd instinctively, as those desperate to illicit support will look for it anywhere, and realized as immediately that he would not get any support from Tawd. Outing without waiting for an acknowledgement of the transmission was equivalent to hanging up on someone in the middle of a heated phone call.

It was rude.

And what hurt most was that Tamara had been the one who outed him.

"My shift," he muttered, "alright."

He marched to the tool room with Tawd chuckling in the background.

Chapter Twenty-Seven: Explanation

The screech of the engines quieted as Tamara sealed the engine room door. She took off her ear defenders and turned to hang them on her hook. She jumped noticing Julian, arms crossed, standing beside the tool bench, waiting.

"So this is how it's going to be now?" he asked in an accusatory tone.

She huffed, reached around him, and hung the ear defenders on her hook.

"You use the radio to broadcast your indignance?" he said.

"We are not friends," Tamara said. "This—"

Julian guffawed. "Wow, do you ever sound like Tawd."

She rolled her eyes. "Ooo, owe, you got me. Is that supposed to be a bad thing?" She set her elbows bent, a hand on each hip. She opened her mouth and pushed out her lower jaw. Her head titled, forcing her eyes to look up to keep contact with Julian. "I'm waiting," she said. Then she scoffed. "You forget that I've known Tawd longer than I've known you. We were doing real activism while you were still whining in the Faroes. He might be a little bit extreme, but I'll take extreme any day over what you are. Coward. Cis. I should have never helped you in your little scheme. I'm so stupid. I should have never let you—inside me! You make me sick. You know that? And your little hard-on for Tawd; give me a break. You just don't like him because of his sincerity, because of his passion, because his dedication to the Legion exposes your lie." She laughed. "You're not Trident Legion. You're a wannabe. A poseur." She shook her head. "You're a loser, Julian."

Julian's demeanour collapsed. Not because Tamara had called him a loser or accused him of being a coward. It wasn't for anything that she said in her tirade. No. Julian deflated because suddenly everything became clear.

"Did you tell Tawd that I poured those buckets overboard?"

Tamara's eyebrows jumped. She looked like a child caught in a fib. But that was it. As quickly as they'd jumped, her eyebrows returned to normal, laissez-faire with a so-what flare. She shrugged. "And then we told the captain."

Her smug smile hurt Julian more than what she was saying.

"And just a heads up, not that you deserve it, but I want you to hear it from me direct: The Captain is kicking you off the crew when we get to San Diego." She pugged her smile. "You'll never get a spot on another ship again."

And with that, she skipped out of the room and left Julian standing stunned, alone, not smiling at all.

Chapter Twenty-Eight: Assertion

For the next eight hours, Julian monitored the gauges. He kept an eye on the temporary seal for a leak, and otherwise when not patrolling the engine room he stared blankly at the mauve dimpled tool room walls.

As he stared, he thought, and as he thought, he realized: he was exhausted.

The weight of five months of being pushed around by the sea, elated one moment, depressed the next, pull in a net—its clean—life is good; come across a dead animal—it's the end of the world. Up and down multiple times a day. His nerves were shot. He didn't know what he expected the campaign would be like, but he knew it wasn't this.

He reasoned to himself. The captain wants to kick him off the ship. She wants to kick him out of the Legion. Okay. Whatever. She can't if he's already gone.

He looked around the tool room. The multi-driver on the wall beamed at him. So did the headlamp, and the yellow-handled serrated Myerchin blade, and the braided carabiner attached to the reserve radio above the tool chest. Those would all make decent souvenirs.

A moment later he slapped his own cheek.

"What's gotten into you," he scolded, quietly, to himself.

He wasn't going to steal anything. He wasn't a thief. Not even the St. John's Ambulance first-aid kit under his desk. He felt ashamed at even thinking so. But only for a second.

"Tawd!"

He jumped up from his slump. He remembered poor old Tawd, sick and alone and lying on his bunk in the engineer cabin.

He hurried out of the tool room and through the mess.

Outside his cabin, he paused. There was laughter behind the door. A man and a woman. Tamara for sure. He'd recognize her laugh anywhere. The man was Tawd. Julian ground his teeth. Tawd.

He pushed open the door with such force, if anybody had been standing behind it, they would have been knocked over or clipped so hard the impact would have left a bruise. The door thwapped against the support post in the middle of the cabin.

Tamara sprang from where she sat at the end of the mattress. "Jesus, Julian!"

He stood beside the desk, and in his mind, towered over the two occupants. His hand snapped wide to his side. His outstretched finger pointed through the door

"Out," he said firmly.

The two of them stared amusedly at Julian.

"You're really going to make Tawd move in the state he's in?" Tamara scolded.

Julian didn't blink. "I mean if I'm the one who killed those dolphins, why wouldn't I?"

Tamara's jaw dropped. He thought maybe he'd have to help lift it closed again. Her eyes darkened. Behind her, Tawd clawed up to his elbows. With a voice inflamed by hours of retching, Tawd said in throaty effort, "You're a dead man." And meant it.

Julian didn't flinch. "Out of my cabin. Now."

Tamara stood up and offered Tawd a hand. Together, they shuffled past Julian, both casting venom stares into his soul.

Julian closed the door behind them. He locked it, and in sliding the bolt closed, he realized his hand was shaking. Not just shaking, his hand shook violently. He gripped it tight to his chest. With the back of his legs, Julian felt for the chair and collapsed into it. His heartbeat rose up his breastplate and threatened arrhythmic arrest. He felt the room going black as it had on the bridge, but in remembering then, he gasped a breath and then another, and soon, he was breathing heavy, full breaths, and no longer shaking where he sat.

He didn't kill those dolphins and he knew he hadn't. But he also knew that saying so as cold matter-of-fact as he had, was exactly what he needed to do if only to get them to leave. Those dolphins were dead long before they surfaced. Anybody with half a discerning brain could see that. He rested his head on the desk. After some time he opened his locker and evaluated its contents. His prize possession rested on the top shelf. The conch shell from the day the crew combed the beach outside the harbour, collecting trash and debris to beautify the coastline. It was their act of goodwill, but more importantly an opportunity for a media post. 'Trident Legion volunteers clean native shoreline,' ching-ching-ching, the little cash register would chime. But its there he found the beautiful shell.

There was the life vest he was issued when he came aboard. A Trident Legion hoodie, two t-shirts, the official campaign shirt and a pair of black embroidered overalls. All of those were given to him when he joined the crew and held no sentimental clinging after all the crap he'd experienced.

On the side shelf, neatly spaced and meticulously organized, his toothbrush, toothpaste, deodorant, and nail clippers lay in a row. Behind them, his clear toiletries travel bag. Julian scooped up his toiletries and deposited them inside. Next he removed his ultra-light Osprey backpack and stowed the little bag in one of the outside pockets. He removed both pairs of shorts, both non-Trident Legion t-shirts, both pairs of socks and both pairs of underwear that he had brought with him those many months ago, and tucked them strategically into the main pouch. Julian set the conch shell on top of his clothing, and his towel on top of the shell. Julian retrieved his journal from the shelf above the desk and slipped that into the bag as well. Then he zipped the bag shut.

He looked around the cabin to see if he'd forgotten anything. On the clothes line strung across the ceiling hung his bathing suit. He grabbed that and tucked the blue material into a side pocket of his bag. When he was satisfied that he'd gathered up everything and that he wasn't leaving anything behind he returned his backpack to the locker and closed its doors.

He still needed to get his passport from the bridge; the captain collected everybody's passport when they boarded; and if he was up there anyway, he'd have Ed sign his sea log, even though he didn't plan on ever being back on a Trident Legion ship. That would be his proper souvenir. Something he had earned; more or less at least.

Chapter Twenty-Nine: Resolution

For the remaining days Julian wore only issued Trident Legion swag and nothing of his own. All of his personal belongings were safety packed inside his backpack and stowed inside his locker. When the first chance to walk presented itself he would take it, no second thoughts. Until then, it was head down, do his job, and bring the ship in safe. At least that was the plan. Compared to everything that had happened over these past few months, Julian knew that the plan never really played out accordingly. Still, he hoped, maybe, just maybe, King Triton would grant him this one wish.

He wasn't surprised when Ed stopped by the tool room one morning and told him to pop up to his cabin when he had a minute. The way everybody on the crew seemed to be ignoring him, he figured the rumour mill had been hard it again and all the blame over those rotted dolphins were netted completely over Julian's shoulders. Even the captain seemed to be avoiding him. If she needed anything done by the engineers, it had become a direct to Tamara request.

Julian set away his gear and climbed the stairs to Ed's cabin.

On the abnormally large cedar computer desk beside the weathered industrial laptop bouncing "Get 'er done," around the black screen, was an officially stamped paper clipped to his his blue jacket gold embossed Canadian passport.

Ed sat on his bed. He motioned Julian to the chair by the sink.

"Have a seat buddy," Ed said.

Julian complied, looking around the room, finding it remarkably small and disbelieving only a few nights earlier that he, Ed, Lisa, Ben, and Jessie had all crammed into this space to celebrate the success of their secret mission.

"I see you grabbed my passport for me," Julian said, not too friendly but not insubordinate either.

"I printed off your sea log, too. Stamped it official and all that so if you ever want to use it for a job or anything, it's good to go." He forced a smile.

"I didn't kill those Vaquita, Ed," Julian said. "You know that, right?"

"It doesn't matter what I know, Julian. It matters what it looks like. You know that. That's all any of this is. A matter of appearance. In the Faroe's, here, Trident Legion has to maintain face."

"So you're kicking me off?"

"Do you really want to stay?"

Julian bit his knuckle.

"Nobody on the crew is going to say anything to anyone outside the ship. The media team is already reporting their attack on us, the fire at our slip in the harbour, how we stayed as long as we could, and as we were leaving the refuge we came across PROFEPA and the navy trying to cover up the death of four more Vaquita as a result of abandoned gill nets."

"But that's what happened."

"Yeah, but that's not all that happened."

"You're telling me that a gallon of sludge contributed to their dying. They were rotted like all the dead fish we've recovered from those nets."

"You poured oil overboard, Julian."

"We were taking on water."

"Convince the die-hards down there. Oil is oil is oil. And you poured it into the ocean, straight into the habitat of this campaign's sole object-ive."

"So I was supposed to let us sink."

"You were supposed to not get caught."

Ed's words hung thick between the two friends.

"This isn't the life for everyone," Ed offered.

"Everything is so messed up," Julian said.

"It's been quite the trip though, hasn't it?" Ed grinned. "I mean could you have ever imagined?"

Julian shook his head. He looked up at Ed and grinned.

"No," he said.

"How many people get to say they've done what you have? Forget this place. You're young. Go have fun. Try something new. You're not married to the Legion. You can change your mind about things."

"I wouldn't say that too loud."

Ed chuckled. "I'm not joking. Try something and see if it works for you. Change it when it doesn't. It's called adulting." He offered Julian his hand. "We good?"

Julian raised his eyes and clasped Ed's hand. "We're good."

"We're almost home. Just keep doing what you've been doing, we'll bring the ship in safe, and you'll be off on your next adventure. Alright?"

"Too easy."

Chapter Thirty: San Diego

And it was. When the American shoreline became visible the deck doors were reopened. The fresh air quickly forced out all the stale green air of the under cabin. Anyone who was bedridden suddenly found their legs. The crew rushed to the deck and leaned over the stanchions. Everybody smiled. It wasn't five minutes upon breaching the deck surface that cellphones started chiming on. Arms raised and turned in slow circles. The crew rushed to capture a single bar and in doing so, communicate with the people waiting on shore. The cliques that had formed during campaign took selfie pictures of themselves, then, because everybody was friends and part of the collective group, started taking pictures of each other and all. After an hour of hubris, Lisa instructed her deck crew to put on clean gear and get ready for the welcoming party.

Passerby's waited to watch the M/V Edward Abbey steer into the harbour. Cameras shuttered with excitement, flashes flashed, everybody waved.

On deck, Lisa's team wore clean Trident Legion gear and adorned proud smiles. The media team stood on the fly deck and captured the spectacle. The world wouldn't know about the mishaps because there was no digital documentation of any of the mishaps. The Trident Legion had been forced to abandon their campaign. The image was so carefully curated, only smiles and waves, only victories or playing the victim was allowed to circulate beyond the ship. If a hundred animals were saved, send it out. If an ancient turtle was killed by an abandoned net, market it. Sink three trawlers, half-a-dozen fishing boats—never happened. Sneak into town and provoke the locals by damaging their gear—the tools they used to earn their livelihoods, the tools they used to feed their families—deny, deny, deny. Here, look at this mountain of nets we recovered. Why, you wonder, does it say Parley on the bag? Don't worry, they were donated, just like you can donate today.

A 10News San Diego van was parked on the pier, its satellite pointed skyward and video team recording the homecoming. A paid advertising slot. Over the next week, Trident Legion would be hosting tours aboard the ship. Campaign gear and reclaimed floats and handcrafted jewellery from the hooks retrieved from long lines pulled from the ocean would be sold—all proceeds allotted to fund the next campaign. Donations welcomed and encouraged.

When the captain was certain the cameras were rolling, she tugged the air horn twice and elicited a cheer from shore. The sun reflected off all the enamel hulls of all the million-dollar yachts in the harbour. It was a far cry from the rusted trawlers in San Felipe. The slips were swept free of debris, all the mooring lines were neatly coiled. Even the trash bins, located at the junctions connecting the various gangways to all the other boats were polished bright. For a mile in each direction, pristine boats, outboards and inboards and sailboats and yachts—mega yachts, with dedicated crews to maintain the idle engines for when their owners decided to afternoon in the San Diego bay—bobbed in the glass marina waters.

From the clubhouse, overlooking all the boats, women in white widebrim hats, men in polo shirts and athletic sunglasses, children with puzzled faces, stared at the rusted hull, the chipped paint, and the weathered bow of the M/V Edward Abbey as it motored into its slip at the centre of the marina.

One week is what the marina could offer. One week until a space in the dry docks would open up to get the Abbey in for repairs. One week was not in the cards for Julian.

Docked, he killed the engines, switched the power from the generators to the dock supplied lode, squared away everything in the tool room, and retreated to his cabin.

The crew had been given the night off to enjoy the marina's amenities: take a shower, have a hot meal in the restaurant, go for swim in the pool or a soak in the hot tub. It was time to enjoy all the superfluous pleasures of the high life. All the things the crew had voluntarily stripped them-selves of, to serve the ocean. They'd earned it. And quickly indulged.

Julian sat in the swivel chair at his computer desk. The cursor blinked what it always blinked, at the end of the sentence of the handover report about the busted seal beneath the starboard engine.

The busted elbow which leaked all the water that filled the bilge.

The oily-water he dumped overboard to keep the Abbey and its crew from sinking.

The good intention which became the backdrop for the four floating Vaquita and staked a gash between him and Tamara.

The captain's words, "Why didn't you deal with that as soon as you came on board," rattled around his skull.

Julian sighed.

He pulled off his tattered Trident Legion shirt, stared at the skull and trident and staff for a while, then tossed it on his bunk.

He retrieved his backpack from his locker, pulled out a clean t-shirt and shorts, then zipped it closed. With nothing he came, and with nothing he would leave. Julian crept out of his cabin, climbed the ladder beside his door to the fore deck, looked around so not to cross anyone's path and scaled the accommodation ladder to the dock.

Having left the ship, he didn't look back. And this was adulting.

THE END

Acknowledgements

Many individuals have contributed to the development of this novel. I would especially like to thank Dr. Kayleigh Moore of the University of Gloucestershire who helped develop an earlier version of this story. I also wish to thank The Cobalt Weekly and The Dalhousie Review where some of these chapters first appeared.